I0620347

The Marlboro Man

BOOK 2 OF THE
MEN OF THE SPRAWLING A RANCH SERIES

BY

ANNA ALEXANDER

http://annaalexander.net/

House of Rosenorn
The Marlboro Man

ISBN: 978-0-9905955-3-3
ALL RIGHTS RESERVED

The Marlboro Man Copyright © 2015 Anna Alexander
Print Edition

Edited by Gwen Hayes. Copy Edit by Eilis Flynn
Cover design by April Rickard with Dewpoint Studios
Cover photography by Jenn LeBlanc with Studio Smexy,

Book publication February 2015

With the exception of quotes used in reviews, this book may not be reproduced or used in whole or in part by any means existing without written permission from the publisher, House of Rosenorn

Warning: The unauthorized reproduction or distribution of this copyrighted work is illegal. No part of this book may be scanned, uploaded or distributed via the Internet or any other means, electronic or print, without the publisher's permission. Criminal copyright infringement, including infringement without monetary gain, is investigated by the FBI and is punishable by up to 5 years in federal prison and a fine of $250,000. (http://www.fbi.gov/ipr/). Please purchase only authorized electronic or print editions and do not participate in or encourage the electronic piracy of copyrighted material. Your support of the author's rights is appreciated.

This book is a work of fiction and any resemblance to persons, living or dead, or places, events or locales is purely coincidental. The characters are productions of the author's imagination and used fictitiously.

The publisher and author acknowledge the trademark status and trademark ownership of all trademarks, service marks and word marks mentioned in this book.

The publisher does not have any control over, and does not assume any responsibility for, author or third party websites or their content.

For years Mark Webber was in love with his best friend's girl, and it had become well past time for him to move on for greener pastures. Not long after he left, Mark realized the Sprawling A was his home, so now he's back, ready to leave the past in the dust. While he was gone, there had been some changes at the A, including a new ranch hand who comes with a sister that stirs Mark's passions in ways he never felt.

Gabriella Montoya has come to the ranch seeking shelter after a failed marriage. Not only is she welcomed with open arms, but she gains six big brothers. But one man doesn't look at her like he would a sister. Oh, no. Mark gazes at her with a heat and promise in his eyes, and damn if he doesn't deliver on every one. But Gabriella's not certain she's ready to embark on another relationship so soon with a man who has made no bones about wanting forever, especially when both of their pasts rise from the ashes and threaten everything they have.

DEDICATION

Para mi familia. Siempre.

Acknowledgements

It takes a village to put a book together, and my village consists of two fantastic editors who work hard to make my words shine. Gwen Hayes and Eilis Flynn, I thank you for making me a stronger writer

FIND ANNA ONLINE

Website
http://annaalexander.net/

Facebook
https://www.facebook.com/pages/Anna-Alexander/282170065189471?ref=hl

Twitter
https://twitter.com/AnnaWriter

Newsletter
http://eepurl.com/Q0tsz

Chapter One

N O MATTER HOW much Mark concentrated, there was no way in hell a stick of spearmint gum was gonna replace a long, smooth drag off a Marlboro cigarette.

Snap.

"God, you're getting moody in your old age," Melody huffed and leaned back in the Adirondack chair by his side.

Yep. Sometimes, thirty-two felt ancient.

He slid his sister a lengthy sideways glare before turning his attention back to the clear, star-filled sky. All he had wanted was to enjoy a nice quite evening out on his porch with nothing but the breeze and an occasional flick of a cow's tail to disturb the silence. Then Melody arrived out of the blue, clearly pissed off about something but being all girlie and refusing to come right out and say what it was that put the burr in her saddle. Well, fat chance getting him to play twenty questions to find out why.

Her long red fingernails ticked out a rhythmic beat on the chair's wide wooden arm. The cadence grated off tune with the chirping crickets that surrounded the front porch. From the corner of his eye, he saw her gaze narrow and her lips purse as she stared. And stared. And stared some more. Melody had learned from the best when it came to wearing a person down. Him.

Click, click, click. Click, click, click. Click, click, click.
Snap.

"What do you want, Mel?" he rumbled.

"What do *I* want?" she squeaked in indignation and placed a hand on her chest. "You mean I can't just stop by to visit my big brother? The brother who disappeared for almost a month and then popped back into town two weeks ago and never once said a word to me about it?"

Mark stifled his sigh and continued to snap his gum. "I had to get away for a while."

"No shit."

"Hey, watch your language."

She stuck out her tongue before socking him in the arm. Hard. The emerald in her ring dug into the muscle, sending a numbing zing down his arm.

"Ow! What the hell, Melody?" He opened and closed his palm in an attempt to get the feeling back in his fingers. He probably shouldn't have taught her that trick, but he had to hand it to her, she was an excellent student.

"You scared me," she snapped. "You rarely leave town. Trey just got back from the hospital and then you split? You would never do that, which means something bad happened."

Something happened, all right.

Melody latched onto his forearm and squeezed tight. "Please, Mark. I know you'd rather eat manure than share your feelings, but you need to talk to someone. If you keep it all bottled up, you're going to have a heart attack and die like Dad or wither up like Trey. Please, let me be there for you."

Mark looked into her dark, pleading eyes and his cool exterior cracked as the corners of her mouth drew down in concern. Despite her tendency toward brattiness, he really did love his baby sister and hated to cause her concern.

He sighed and turned his gaze back out into the night. "Trey found out I was in love with Greta."

"Ohhh," she murmured in a long stunned breath.

She was surprised? Really? He never told a soul about his infatuation with his best friend's wife, but Melody was a smart girl. At some point she must have suspected he had feelings for one of her closest friends.

"What did Trey do?" she asked. "What did he say? Does Greta know?"

"He didn't say much of anything." He shrugged. "He had a lot going on at the time."

Like regaining his memory.

Trey's hard climb out of his depression was quite a miracle, actually. And Mark was truly happy for his friend, even if it meant his darkest secret of being in love with Greta was revealed in the process.

Oh, he knew his affections had always been one-sided. Greta loved her husband. Even when Trey withdrew into his mind, shutting everyone out, she held out hope that one day the Trey she remembered would return. And Mark loved her enough to give her the support she had needed, painful as that was.

Now the couple was living their happily ever after. And Mark was left out in the cold.

"When Trey and Greta worked things out, I figured it was time to move on. Give them some time to themselves and go build a life of my own."

"Wait. You planned on never coming back?" Melody gasped. "Never ever?"

"That was the plan. I headed to Tacoma first. Visited with Mom for a few days. She kept going on about why you haven't found a man yet." Melody's lips grimaced into a half smile, but her eyes remained troubled. "What was I going to do, Mel? Stay here and wish for something that was never going to happen? Stand by and watch while they… I had to—I had to—"

He reached into his front pocket and drew out the pack of gum that replaced his Marlboros. He had started smoking years ago to keep his hands and mind off of Greta. With that dream gone, he figured it was a good time to do a clean sweep of his life and quit. Another one of his bonehead ideas.

Silver paper crinkled between his fingers as he replaced the flavorless piece he'd been chewing. The muscles in his jaw ached as he worked the fresh stick between his teeth. He went through so much of the stuff, he was probably spending more on gum in one day than he ever had on cigarettes.

"So what brought you back?" his sister asked.

Nothing and everything.

He had flown out of town without a clue as to what to do next. He spent the first week losing himself in booze and women, stupidly thinking he could bury his yearnings for Greta between silky thighs and bottles of beer. But all the partying did was teach him two things.

One-night stands made him feel dirty.

And he hadn't been in love with Greta.

Yeah, when he reached that realization, it about knocked him on his ass, but it was true. Greta was the first woman he had met with all of the attributes he wanted in a wife, but she was always meant for Trey. A truth he came to terms with when his smile didn't feel so forced and the longing to return grew so great, the thought of seeing the lovebirds again didn't burn a hole in his gut. He knew then it was time to come home to the ranch.

He tapped the back of Melody's hand. "You brought me back. And Trey, and even Greta. She's great, and I still care for her, but those two are made for each other. They're good together. Especially when Trey has his head out of his ass." He winked. Melody's shoulders relaxed, and for the first time that night, she offered him a genuine smile. "Nowhere I went felt right, Mel. I've been working this land and these cows since I was twelve. All of my friends are here, and you, my bratty sister. This is my home."

"I'm glad you came back. I missed you." She sniffed once and turned her profile to him. "Even though you're a jerk."

A tickle of guilt stirred in his chest. Well, shit, she really had been worried about him. When he had left, escape had been the only thing on his mind. He never thought twice about giving Melody a heads up. For a sister, she was pretty decent about giving him his space. Now he saw just how selfish his actions had been.

He reached out and squeezed her hand. "I'm sorry I worried you. I won't do it again," he promised.

"Good." She sniffed again and tossed a lock of her black hair over her shoulder. "With you not being here, I ran out of reasons to come hang out. There were only so many excuses I could come up with to visit Greta and check out the new ranch hand. Wow, is he hot." She shot him a sly smile.

In Melody speak, her teasing meant he was forgiven, but his brow still furrowed at her words.

She relaxed in her chair and drew up a knee. "He's so handsome and mysterious. And I just love his name. Rafael Montoya. Isn't it dreamy?"

"I want you to stay away from him."

Her dark brows popped up in surprise. "Why? You hired him."

"I didn't hire him. Trey did when Steven left for college. He's a good hand, but—" he almost said, "too much for you to handle," but held his tongue. He'd already pissed her off enough.

"I don't want you getting all flirty with any of the hands."

With an unladylike snort, she stood and crossed over to the railing. "Stop treating me like a child." Leaning far over the rail, she looked down the lane toward the house that Rafael shared with Jack and Adam. "Do you think the boys are home? Maybe they're up for a game of poker?"

"Do you want me to take you over my knee and paddle you?"

Her lips curled into a devilish smile. "I would love to have Rafael paddle me." Her nose crinkled every time she trilled out his name. It was more than annoying. "I can just imagine being laid over his lap and feeling his big hard—"

"Hey!" He shot to his feet. "Watch your mouth. I don't want to hear that coming from you." The thought of his sister connected to anything sexual gave him the willies.

Her evil laugh did little to console him. In two steps, she had her arms wrapped around his waist and hugged him tight. "I'm glad you're home."

He tightened his hold and ran his hand down the length of her hair. "Me too, brat."

She gave him another squeeze and drew back. "I should go. I'll let you catch up on your beauty sleep. Looks like you could really use some."

"Did I actually think I missed you?" He smiled at her frown and threw his arm around her shoulders. "I'll walk you out. Don't want you taking any detours."

"You're such a fuddy-duddy." She pouted and clomped down the porch steps.

"At least *I'm* not using the word 'fuddy-duddy.' What are you, ninety?"

She kicked gravel in his direction and laughed again. Her car was parked in the circular driveway at the end of the lane. To their left was the main house of the Armstrong clan. A porch light glowed a soft yellow in welcome, but Mark knew Trey and Greta had gone out for the evening. It seemed as if everyone had plans that night but him.

Melody opened the car door and set one foot inside. "Tell Greta I'll call her later. And say hi to *Rrrrafael* for me," she added before ducking in and shutting the door.

"You're not funny," he called out. Through the windshield he saw her shoulders shaking and the white of her teeth as she laughed. "Brat," he muttered, even as the corner of his mouth lifted into a grin.

Like a good watchful brother, he waited until her taillights faded in the distance before he started back toward his house. The three-bedroom, two-story farmhouse had been the original homestead for the Sprawling A until the main house was built in the early 1900s. It then became the home of the ranch foreman, with more than enough room for a wife and a couple of kids. If Mark ever got that lucky.

About a dozen steps down the road, he paused as the sound of tires on gravel caught his attention. Did Melody forget something, he wondered and glanced back down the drive.

Nope, the headlights coming down the lane were too low to be Melody's Ford Escape, and the purr of the engine much too quiet to be Trey's monster truck. It was either a girl out looking for one of the hands or someone had really lost their way.

Mark waited under the one light that illuminated the driveway. His curiosity grew when a silver Mercedes pulled to a stop a few feet away. In this neck of the woods, people drove trucks, SUVs, or tractors. Whoever was driving was most definitely not from the area.

The figure inside shifted around for a few minutes before the door opened and a dainty foot in a three-inch heel emerged, followed by a shapely leg encased in flesh-colored nylons that shimmered in the low light. His heart began to pound and he almost swallowed his gum.

"Jim-in-y," he breathed out slowly when she finally turned to face him.

Chapter Two

I F HE HAD been asked to put together his fantasy woman, this girl would have had all of his favorite parts and then some. Mark blinked hard and bit the inside of his cheek to make sure he wasn't dreaming.

The mystery woman stood in the driveway, partially hidden in the shadows. Her pale skin glowed with an ethereal blue radiance in the moonlight. Dark hair spilled over her shoulders like a waterfall and made him wonder if she was wearing some of those fake hair things. The fine silk blouse she wore pulled tight over her large breasts, straining the button holding the fine fabric together. Generous hips complemented her perfect hourglass figure.

Mark's palms itched to latch onto her and pull her tight against him just to see if she felt as lush as she looked. Despite the chill in the air, a fine sheen of sweat collected above his lip. The deep steadying breath he took carried her floral citrus scent and woke up every cell in his body.

Who was this woman?

"Can I—" he stopped to clear his throat. "Can I help you?"

"I'm looking for Rafael Montoya," she replied. Her gaze darted all around before coming back to him.

Disappointment rode him hard even as the sound of the

other man's name trilling off her tongue sent a shudder down his spine. Of course she was here for Rafe. Ever since the good-looking Latino set foot on the ranch, women had been dropping their panties for him in droves.

If there was one thing Mark prided himself on, it was that he was always a gentleman. Even with the swirl of jealousy stirring a tempest in his gut, he'd do everything he could to assist her. "I saw him set out on one of the bikes a few hours ago. Would you like me to try his radio?"

"Yes, please."

He pulled his Nextel from his belt and dialed Rafe's number.

"It's Mark," he responded when Rafe picked up the call. "There's a lovely lady here to see you. What's your name, miss?" he asked her.

"Gabriella," she replied with that same roll of the tongue she used earlier.

"Gabriella," he repeated, enjoying the way the syllables rolled around in his mouth.

The radio went dead after a hasty "I'll be right there." Mark didn't blame him. If he knew this fine-looking woman was waiting for him, he'd hightail it to her side too.

"He's on his way."

"Thank you," she replied, crossing her arms around her middle. The movement plumped up those magnificent breasts and brought his attention to the fact that she was really cold in the chilly night air.

"My place is just down the way. You're welcome to wait there. I'm Mark Webber. I'm the foreman here." He held out his hand with the hope that she'd come closer. He wanted a better look at her in the light to have a memory to hold on to for later. The only way he'd ever have a shot with a woman this classy was in his dreams.

The tip of her tongue swiped along her lower lip as warily eyed his outstretched hand. The breath froze in his lungs as he waited. He sensed that this was a test of some kind and he wanted to pass.

With a deep breath she lifted her gaze to his and took a step forward. Her gait was awkward as if she were forcing herself to move. The closer she came, the tinier she appeared. She really was just an itty-bitty thing.

"Nice to meet you, Mark." Her firm handshake trembled and her skin was as cold as an ice cube in his warm grip.

He lifted his gaze from their clasped hands to her face and then sucked in a harsh breath as his hand tightened around hers.

Under the bright overhead light, he saw the blue and green bruises she tried to cover with a layer of foundation. No wonder her brown, fathomless eyes watched him like a hawk, why her lithe body was so tense. Her full lower lip reminded him of a ripe strawberry, and it was swollen where it had been split open. More faded bruises graced her throat like a necklace. The marks didn't detract from her exotic beauty, but only emphasized the fact that no woman should ever be touched with such anger.

"Did he do this to you?" he growled. Anger and a thirst for vengeance coursed through his veins.

"What?" she said, confused, before her eyes widened as she realized he could see her injuries. "Rafe? No." She shook her head so her thick hair fell and covered the wounded half of her face. "No, no."

She tugged hard on his fingers, bringing his attention to his crushing grip. "I'm sorry." He dropped her hand like a hot branding iron. Red colored his vision for a moment before he shook his head to clear it. "You're so tiny. I didn't mean to hurt you. Are you all right?" He searched her face for any sign of discomfort.

"I'm fine." Her expression was passive, with no indication that she was anything other than all right.

"Let's get you to where it's warmer." He gestured for her to go ahead. He tamped down the overwhelming urge to sweep her up in his arms for protection. As she passed him, his palm brushed the silk on her lower back to escort her, before he remembered his place and snatched it away.

He had no right touching her or guiding her that way. She didn't belong to him. She wasn't his to care for or avenge. Where was this caveman tendency coming from? She was a stranger. How could this little slip of a woman affect him so quickly? Make his blood boil with a few soft-spoken words?

He exhaled through his noise with a harsh breath and chomped down on his gum with more force than necessary. Jesus, he really needed to stop wanting his friends' women. Ignoring the throbbing below his belt, he kept his focus on the dirt road in front of him and not on the sway of her hips. He'd never thought he would find a tweed skirt so sexy.

Once inside the warmth of his house, he offered her a seat in the overstuffed armchair. She waved him away with an elegant hand. "I'll stand, if that's okay."

"Whatever you want." He left the front door open a crack and then took a position close to the entry to the kitchen, making sure he wasn't between her and the exit. Who knew where she was mentally or what she had gone through. The last thing he wanted was for her to feel trapped or uncomfortable while in his home.

"Have you lived here long?" she asked as she began a slow stroll around the living room. In her fine, tailor-made clothes, she looked out of place amongst the battered leather and wood furniture. She was like a Louis XIV dining table sitting in the middle of a honky-tonk bar.

Her gaze bounced all around, from the wood-paneled walls to the stone fireplace and back to him. The look on her face was not one of judgment, but of watchfulness as she pondered all of the available escape routes. Good girl.

"I've been the foreman for about eight years. Been working the ranch since I was twelve."

"So you grew up in Mission?"

"Yep."

"Then you would know almost everyone here, right? The town doesn't seem that big, so you would know if anyone new started coming around?"

The corner of his mouth kicked up. He had an idea of what she was hinting at. "Out here, the grapevine is faster than the Internet. I'm sure even your arrival tonight will be all the talk at Mindy's Diner come breakfast time."

She released a sigh and a little chuckle as her shoulders relaxed and she appeared to be at ease for the first time since she stepped out of her Mercedes.

Her heels clicked on the hardwood floor as she walked to the bookcase. "She's pretty," she said, picking up one of the photos on display. "Is this your wife?"

He couldn't stop the snort that escaped. "That's my sister, Melody."

"Oh," she said with a laugh. "Sorry." The sight of her smile started a hum buzzing through his body again. He watched in confusion as she opened the bookcase's lower cabinet and placed the photo inside. "You two look like you get along well."

"We live to torment each other." He frowned as she placed the candles Melody had given him years ago in an attempt to add ambiance to the room in the cabinet as well.

"You love her." It wasn't a question. She sounded as if she had experience in how brothers and sisters showed their affections.

"I do. She left a few minutes before you got here. That was why I was outside." Bit by bit, she methodically cleared off every surface of books and mementos and placed them in the cabinet and then closed the door. "Is there a reason why you're hiding my things?"

"Well, my brother—"

"Lita?" A deep voice shouted before the door burst open admitting a tall, lean Latino man. His wide, welcoming grin faded when Gabriella turned to face him.

"Goddamn motherfucker!" he shouted. "Motherfucking fuckhead asshole!"

Mark froze in shock as he watched and listened to the usually level-headed man launch into a string of obscenities in both English and Spanish.

Rafe stomped back and forth in tight circles, the clomp-clomp of his footsteps drowning out his shouts and the occasional angry slap of his riding gloves against the leather of his chaps. His hands clenched and released as if he were choking someone. Mark guessed Rafe was imagining whoever hurt Gabriella. He wouldn't mind having a few minutes alone with the bastard himself.

Through all the shouting, Gabriella never moved. The only telltale sign of her emotions was the gradual welling of tears in her eyes. As the cursing grew more fevered, Rafe marched up to the bookshelves and growled when he realized they were empty. He turned around then picked up the remote control, the only object weighing less than thirty pounds and not nailed down, and threw it against the wall.

"Hey!" Mark shouted when the plastic casing clattered to the floor in pieces.

Rafe jerked as if waking from a dream. His chest heaved in

and out as he stared down at the little woman who stood in the eye of the storm.

Her lashes fluttered and one tear spilled free to slide down her cheek. "I love you too," she said.

Her softly spoken words appeared to vent the pressure of Rafe's rage. His shoulders slumped as all of his bluster dissipated like a balloon with the end lopped off. In two strides, he was on her, pulling her into a tight embrace and rocking her back and forth as his hand brushed over her hair, slow and easy. Over the top of her head Rafe met Mark's gaze. "Hey, boss. Could I have a few minutes alone with my sister?"

Chapter Three

THROUGH LOWERED LASHES, Gabriella observed the man who was Rafe's boss. He wasn't a huge man by any stretch of the imagination, but he definitely looked like he could hold his own in a tough situation. Actually, he was built a lot like Rafe, with that same lean muscular stature that spoke of years working with animals and lugging hay bales. Broad chest and shoulders, small waist, and strong thighs. Very masculine.

When she had spotted him in the driveway upon her arrival, his strong chin and watchful gaze gave him a menacing look that triggered a knee-jerk reaction for her to hide in the shadows. How long would he have stood there, watching her with that curious frown on his face, before she managed to pull her head out of her scaredy-cat ass?

Someday, someday soon, she vowed, her brain wouldn't label every man she met as a possible attacker. If she'd wanted to live in fear for the rest of her life, she would have stayed with her ex-husband.

Those dark eyes of his watched them as her brother rocked her from side to side. No hint of his thoughts showed on his face as he nodded. "I'll be down the hall if *either* of you need me."

She hid her smile in Rafe's shirt. Her brother was usually the calm, proverbial rock of the family—until someone he loved was threatened. Then he turned into a Tasmanian devil and destroyed everything in his path. By the way Mark looked as he spoke of his sister, she had a suspicion he'd behave the same way.

Once Mark's heavy footsteps faded down the hall, Rafe set her away from him. "I'll kill him, Lita. I swear to God, if I see him, he's dead."

"Don't." She placed a hand on either side of his tan face and drew his attention on her. "He's not worth it. Besides, he knows too many lawyers. Please. I need you here."

"Gabriellita," he said, sighing, and briefly closed his eyes. Pinching her chin between his thumb and forefinger, he tilted her face to the left and right, assessing her bruises. "Tell me this was the only time." When she looked away, he gritted his teeth. "Tell me everything. What happened?"

Where did she begin? More pressing, how much should she divulge to her overprotective big brother? So much anger rolled off Rafe, the serenity she had spent the last few months trying to obtain threatened to evaporate like a raindrop in the sun. The temptation was there to crack and fall back into the morass of helplessness, but that wasn't why she sought him out.

She stepped away from his brewing ire and rubbed her palms up and down her arms. "About eight months ago, we were going to a fundraiser and Drew wanted me to wear an outfit I thought was too revealing. We argued, and he slapped me."

She shook her head of the painful memory of that moment when her husband's open hand hit her cheek. "He apologized. Said that he was stressed out with work and that all he wanted was to spend a nice evening showing off his pretty wife. He begged for my forgiveness and promised to never do it again. He even bought me diamond earrings." Tears filled her eyes with the reminder that she had been bought off with a piece of sparkle.

"But he did hit you again. Didn't he?" Rafe growled.

Not right away. For several weeks, Drew had been the model of a perfect husband. Then the snide comments about what she ate and the clothes she wore went from occasional to every day. Her husband's family—well, he and his mother, anyway—had a very specific image they wanted them to project. Successful, perfect, willing to do anything to get ahead.

Or anyone.

The end had come when one of Drew's clients had made a pass at her at a party. They had been celebrating the closing of a real estate deal, and his client told her Drew could go far if she spent the weekend naked and tied to his bed. The suggestion itself hadn't shocked her so much as the suggestion was made with Drew standing right beside her, and even worse, her husband had encouraged her to take the offer. When she refused, the menacing look he had given her had sent a spike of fear through her chest.

All evening long she hoped that the entire situation was a misunderstanding or a cruel joke taken too far, but that hope was crushed in the angry grip of Drew's fist when they had returned home.

"You are mine!" he had shouted at her after striking her twice. Sweat and spit had dripped on her huddled, shaking form. "That ring on your finger marks you as mine. If I tell you to fuck every man in my office, you will do so. Do you understand?"

She could only whimper under the bruising force of his hand around her neck. Every kind thought or loving feeling she ever had about Drew Daws died that night.

All through breakfast the next morning, she had sat quietly while he read his paper with a smug smile on his face. Five minutes after he left for a golf date, she packed a bag and went right to the police.

Rafe touched her arm and brought her back to the present. She cleared her throat again. "When he… uh, the second time, I went to the police and pressed charges. They took pictures and tests. He was arrested that night. Of course, he posted bail."

"Damn it, Lita, you should have called me."

"I didn't want to bother you. You were on the move with the Jangula family and settling into the new arena."

"That was four months ago," he shouted then sucked in his outrage when she winced. "Why did you wait so long? And why are you bruised now? Did that fucker come after you again?"

"The no-contact order is against Drew. Not his mother's butler. This was their way of trying to talk me into dropping the charges and going back to him."

"Tell me that motherfucker is now in jail."

She shook her head.

"Motherfucker—"

"There weren't any witnesses, and they'd only claim I was making things up. Look, Rafe, I didn't mean to show up and dump my troubles on you, but I don't feel safe anywhere else, and I took so little when I had left Drew, and now… I just—I just—" The adrenaline high she had been riding since going on the run crashed and the crumbled remnants of what her life had become left her shaking.

"Don't you for one second think you're dumping anything on me. You should have come to me six months ago." He gave her shoulders a little shake before dragging her close to hug her tight. "You're safe here, Lita. I'll protect you."

She squeezed him back before stepping away to wipe at her eyes. She was so sick of crying. After the police collected their evidence that first night, she had cried for three hours solid while standing under the shower's spray, then again after each time she spoke with the detectives. The time for crying was officially over, and from now on her focus was going to be on getting her shit together. The bastard didn't deserve any more of her time.

"So what happens now?" Rafe asked. "They're just gonna let him walk?"

"No. The trial is in two months. I was hoping to hang out in Mission until I'm due back in court. I didn't feel safe in the studio I was renting."

"You'll stay as long as you need. Trial or no trial. Hey, Mark!" he called toward the doorway.

Mark entered the room on silent feet. The black in his eyes glittered with darkness as a muscle ticked in his jaw. His lips were pressed so tight together they appeared white.

Judging by his dark look, she guessed he heard every word they said. She suspected as much. As the foreman, it was probably his job to ferret out any potential trouble that could be brought to the ranch.

Would he judge her? Think her shallow for accepting gifts that were clearly bribes? All of her so-called friends turned their backs on her when she left Drew. They indicated with their actions and not-so-subtle comments that she'd be crazy to turn away from the lifestyle Drew provided. As if she were incapable of having a good life on her own.

Then there were those who thought she was somehow to blame. That she should have known better than to stay and given him that second chance. At times, it seemed that everywhere she turned she was damned if she did and damned if she didn't.

"My sister needs to hide out from a bastard ex-husband." Leave it to Rafe to get right to the point. "Do you think Trey and Greta will let her stay in the main house? I don't want Jack or Adam drooling on her if she stays with me."

"Rafe, no," she protested. "I don't want to impose on strangers. I can stay at a motel."

"It's all right, Gabriella," Mark answered. His cool, calm, and in-control mask was still present, but his eyes burned with fire. The intensity level on which he vibrated sent chills skipping over her skin. "Stay as long as you want. You'll be safer here with everyone watching out for you. Remember the grapevine?" The corners of his mouth quirked up a little, just the tiniest bit that told her he was trying to be reassuring.

"Thank you." She crossed her arms in an attempt to control the tremble caused by the timbre of his voice.

Get a grip, Gabriella. You cannot be attracted to a stranger who could probably pound Drew into the ground without a second thought. You need sleep. A lot of sleep. Alone sleep.

"Trey and Greta are out now," Mark said. "But I have keys to the main house. We can get you settled, and I'll stay until they get back to let them know you're there."

"I'll stay too," Rafe added.

"Okay," she agreed more readily than she should. At this point, she was way too tired to argue about where she would stay for the night. "If you're sure."

"I'm sure." Mark gestured toward the door. "Let's get your bag."

Gabriella led the way back to her car. As Rafe pulled her suitcase from the truck, headlights came up the long drive. A massive Ford pickup came to a stop in front of the garage. The doors opened to the sound of laughter as a man and a woman spilled out.

The carefree sound pulled at her heart. She and Drew had never laughed like that. Like everything was right in the world and all they would ever need was there in each other's arms. With Drew, their relationship had become a mission to find what more they could have to make them happy.

As she watched the handsome blond man wrap his arm around the petite woman and pull her tightly against his side, the bitter taste of regret coated her tongue as she acknowledged just how shallow her two-year marriage had been.

"How was your evening?" Mark called out.

"Good," the man answered, then shared a secret smile with the woman. "Real good."

Mark nodded. "We were just about to make use of one of your guest rooms. This is Rafe's sister, Gabriella. She's had a lousy week and needs a place to stay for a bit. You can probably guess why Rafe thinks she shouldn't stay in one of the bunk houses."

Gabriella was grateful he didn't elaborate on the details of why exactly she was there.

"Of course. We'd love to have you." The man offered her his hand. "I'm Trey Armstrong, and this is my wife Greta."

She shook hands with both of them. "Nice to meet you. It will only be for a few days."

"No problem." Greta smiled warmly. Her breath caught for a second when she looked Gabriella in the face. "It will be nice to have another woman around here," she finished with a distracted cadence before flicking a quick glance at Trey. "Come on in. I'll show you around."

"Thank you again." Gabriella began to follow Rafe as he went up ahead with her bag. A few feet later, she stopped and turned. "It was nice meeting you, Mark."

His lips softened into a shy smile and the heat in his eyes ignited a smoldering fire inside her. "It was nice meeting you too. I'll see you in the morning, Gabriella."

Her mouth went dry at the promise in his gaze. She could only nod and then walked into the house, feeling warmer than she had in a long, long while.

Chapter Four

M ARK WATCHED GABRIELLA disappear into the house and stifled a sigh. From the moment she stepped foot out of her car, his adrenaline had been going like crazy. From relief at knowing he was lusting after Rafe's sister and not his girlfriend, to the anger at the ex who treated her like a punching bag. Not only did he find her courage to take a stand against the abuse admirable but, to his surprise, sexy as hell.

Now she was going to be on the ranch. Every day. With her supermodel hair and stiletto heels. Every day. Within perfume smelling distance away. Every day.

Where were his Marlboros when he needed them?

Trey turned to face him. "So. Rafe's sister, huh?"

"Yep."

"Who hit her?" he asked, a spark of anger glittered in his blue eyes.

"An acquaintance of her bastard ex-husband. She had him arrested a few months ago and he's awaiting trial. They were sent to talk her out of pressing the case. She arrived a few hours ago with nothing but her car and that suitcase."

Trey took a good glance at the Mercedes and whistled in admiration. The man always did have an appreciation for fine automobiles. He shook his head and returned to the seriousness of the situation. "Do you think he'll come after her?"

"Oh, yeah." Of that Mark had no doubt. A shithead who sent an employee to beat up his wife didn't seem the type to give up easily.

Trey nodded. "She'll be safe here. Plus, Greta will enjoy having another woman around." The light that infused his features as he spoke his wife's name was as brilliant as the sun, and his smile brightened as he looked back at the house.

The hairs on Mark's neck prickled. "What's up, Hoss?"

When Trey turned back, worry darkened his expression. He glanced at the ground before meeting Mark's eyes. "Greta's pregnant."

Mark's heart stopped. As the fall breeze teased at his hair, he waited for that pang of loss and hurt that used to come when it came to anything that had to do with Greta.

It never came.

Holy shit, he really was over her. The breath he held eased out, and his shoulders relaxed. The slow smile that stretched his lips came straight from his heart. "That's great. I'm happy for you."

"Really?"

"Yeah."

"I'm scared shitless, you know?" Trey swallowed hard and his gaze dropped.

Yeah, Mark knew. He knew that Trey was thinking about the death of his son, Luke, a few years earlier. Mark had been there when Greta had screamed that little Luke would not wake up and he had tried everything in his power to save the young boy's life. The day Luke passed had been one of the worst days of his life. Mark couldn't blame his friend for being afraid, not one bit.

"You'll be fine." He placed a firm hand on Trey's shoulder. "You're gonna be a great dad."

"I don't want to fuck anything up or worry too much."

"You won't. You love Greta, right?"

His chin rose a notch. "More than anything."

"Then it's going to be all right. Just remember that." His lips quirked up. "And I'll be there to kick you in the ass if you forget."

Trey laughed. "Thanks, man. Are you sure you're all right about all of this?"

"I told you, I resolved the whole Greta and my feelings thing. I'm happy for you. Really."

"Good. Good." He nodded, his posture deflating. "I'm really glad you're back, man."

"Me too."

Trey looked back at the house again, glancing up at the light on the second story that had turned on while they were talking. When he turned back around there was a speculative gleam in his eyes. "I guess I should make sure our guest is taken care of. Although I'm sure Greta and Rafe have it all under control. Will I see you at breakfast?"

Mark looked up at the light as well. A buzz of excitement centered in his belly. "Yep. Wouldn't miss it."

EXHAUSTION CLAIMED GABRIELLA'S body, but sleep wouldn't come. All night long, she replayed the events that brought her to the tiny town in Central Washington. On and on in a continuous loop her mind churned until it propelled her from the bed to the bathroom where she splashed water on her face in an attempt to clear the cobwebs and prepare for the day.

Where had she gone wrong?

On paper, Drew was such an excellent catch. Handsome, wealthy, able to maintain a stable job. Hadn't she done everything he asked of her? Hadn't she quit her job to focus on volunteering for the causes he was interested in? Hadn't she played nice to his pretentious mother? Hadn't she molded herself into the perfect socialite image? The perfect wife? Where had she gone wrong?

"You didn't," she told her reflection in the bathroom mirror. "You did nothing wrong. And don't you ever give in to the belief that you did."

Determination burned in her eyes as she put the finishing touches on her makeup. The bruises had faded enough that they were only visible under certain lighting. The swelling of her lip was down to almost nothing, and the scab was easily covered with lipstick. When her hair was styled with just the right coverage over her face, she looked almost like her old self. Tired, but recognizable.

It was just before six in the morning when she walked down the stairs and into the huge country kitchen. To the right was a large dining table that easily sat ten, and on the left was a cooking area any restaurant owner would be proud of, with stainless steel appliances and a large gas range that appeared used but well cared for. Fortunately, the coffee maker was front and center on the counter, with a canister of rich grounds and a filter waiting patiently by its side. Gabriella set the maker to brew then leaned against the counter and waited. Caffeine and a long walk outside should help clear her mind and focus on the next step.

"You're up early."

Gabriella jumped with a shriek as Greta entered the kitchen. Her long dark hair was pulled into a ponytail, exposing her glowing, vibrant skin that shouted, "I'm a morning person!" Greta's freshly scrubbed appearance made Gabriella feel cheap and tawdry in comparison with her thick layer of makeup.

"I couldn't sleep," she mumbled and poured herself a cup of

coffee. She cupped the mug with both hands and huddled over the steamy brew as if she could disappear into the dark pool of liquid.

"I can imagine. You must have a lot on your mind." Greta opened the refrigerator and took out two cartons of eggs and an armful of vegetables. She worried her lower lip as she set them on the counter. "Can I ask you a personal question?"

"You can ask. Doesn't mean I'll answer," Gabriella said with maybe a little too much defensiveness.

A laugh escaped as Greta nodded. "Fair enough." The knowledge and concern in her steady gaze pinned Gabriella where she stood, like a straight pin through a butterfly's wing. "You're not going to go back to the man who hit you, are you?"

Gabriella sputtered, the coffee burning a track back up her throat. Apparently, the Armstrong's were straight shooters. Neither of them had asked any questions the night before, so the fact that Greta had zeroed in on her situation was both eerie and disconcerting. What would she have to do to shed that "battered woman" appearance?

From what she gathered from Rafe's emails, his employers were good people, and Gabriella sensed her hostess wasn't trying to be rude in any way, but was genuinely worried about her well being.

She swallowed against the unexpected tide of emotions Greta's worry invoked. She never expected a total stranger to express worry for her. "No. Never."

Greta's shoulders relaxed and she smiled. "That's good. We love Rafe to pieces and I saw last night how afraid he is for you. Hell, I'm worried for you. Trey and I both want you to know that you're welcome here for as long as you need."

"Thanks." She cleared her throat. "Thank you." She set her cup aside, feeling both humbled and out of sorts with the generosity. "Can I help you with anything?"

"Sure. Eggs with sausage and peppers are on the menu this morning. Could you wash and cut up the vegetables?"

"Absolutely." Gabriella began rinsing the peppers and tomatoes in the oversized sink. Soon the women fell into a companionable rhythm as they worked side by side.

"Do you have any idea about what you want to do next?" Greta asked as she started to brown the sausage.

"Not a clue. You know, when I was a kid, all I wanted was to get out of Yakima so bad, I was willing to do almost anything. I don't think I'm cut out for small town living, but I know I don't want to go back to Seattle. I don't know. Maybe I'll leave the state, try something really new."

"What about staying here in Mission?"

She frowned at the suggestion. "Mission's even smaller than Yakima. What would I do here?"

"I don't know." Greta shrugged. "What did you do in Seattle?"

"Smiled pretty and spoke seldom."

Greta paused, the concerned frown back on her face. "Seriously?"

Gabriella kept her head bent over her work. "I was the ultimate hostess who planned all of my ex-husband's parties and fundraisers, besides being the decoration on his arm. I used to work at a country club, working conference services. That was where we met. When we married he said that I no longer needed to work, so I became his social secretary, more or less."

"Well, maybe you could do that here. There's a golf course nearby—they may need someone. Or maybe you can open your own business. You know, there are some cute houses you can rent. When I first moved here, I rented one with my cousin and Mark's sister, Melody." A grin curled her lips. "You know, I was only supposed to be in Mission a few months, but Trey had other ideas."

The love in Greta's eyes when she spoke of her husband made Gabriella's heart sore and her stomach sour.

Had she ever looked like that speaking about Drew, or had she been too infatuated by his bank account and fancy car?

"I'll think about it," Gabriella replied and shook off the emptiness that settled in her chest. "Hey, that's more of a plan than I had five minutes ago."

"Excellent." Greta smiled, then her face fell as the color leeched from her cheeks. Her eyes darted around the room in a panic. "Oh God, oh God." She clapped a hand over her mouth and ran out of the room toward the back of the house.

Gabriella heard the sounds of her retching from the direction of the bathroom. "Greta?" she called. "Are you all right?"

"Yeah," came the feeble response. "I'll be fine. The smell got to me."

Gabriella took command of the stove while Greta took care of her personal business. A steamy cloud of onions, peppers, and sausage hit her in the face as she stirred the vegetables. Whew, the combination did make for quite the heady aroma. A basket of tomatoes hung in the corner, so she picked out a few and chopped them up for a quick salsa.

Greta crept back into the kitchen on shaky legs. She wet a paper towel and pressed it to her pale cheeks. "Sorry about that."

"So…when are you due?" Gabriella asked with a grin.

The woman lit up like a Christmas tree. "July." Then a shadow crossed her face.

"What's wrong?" Gabriella shifted her stance just in case she had to dodge a projectile. "Are you going to be sick again?"

"No, no. It's just that this is a big, big deal." Greta worried her lip while looking down at the paper towel in her hands. "We had a son who passed away a few years ago from an aneurysm. He was two."

Gabriella dropped the spoon in her hand. "Oh my God, Greta. How horrible. I'm so sorry."

"It was horrible. Really horrible." She folded the soggy paper as she shook her head. "Trey didn't take it well. He…mentally…went away for a while. He just couldn't find the heart to care about anything anymore. It's only been recently that he found his smile again. Now with the new baby, I can tell he's scared. I'm scared. There's that fear. What if it happens again?" Her hands rested on the nonexistent bulge of her belly.

"I can't imagine going through anything like that. You're way braver than I am."

Greta shook her head. "I can't imagine going through what you have. Even when Trey treated me like I didn't exist, he never would have thought about laying an unkind hand on me. None of the guys here would."

Gabriella didn't know what to say to that, so she just nodded and kept her head down and concentrated on her work. What she was doing now wasn't bravery. It was pure survival.

"Gabriella." Greta placed her hand on her arm. "I'm glad you came here."

She looked up and met Greta's warm gaze. There was no pity. No accusations. Just compassion and friendship. It had been far too long since she had a friend.

"Me too," she said. She blinked back the moisture pooling in her eyes. And she meant it.

The answering smile faded as Greta's eyes open wide in alarm. "Oh no," she muttered before dashing out.

Gabriella clutched at her tummy in sympathy. "Poor girl."

She searched through the pantry for some crackers. After she located the box, she stepped back into the kitchen and almost dropped them with a surprised gasp.

Well, good morning, sir.

Chapter Five

MARK STOOD IN the entryway, looking way too sexy for seven in the morning. His black shirt emphasized just how broad his shoulders were, and the tight fit of his jeans showed off his muscled thighs and flat stomach. She just knew if she circled his fine form, those jeans would be sculpted to his firm backside like a second skin. If he had a cigarette in his mouth, he'd look like a walking Marlboro ad. That calm mask of his was still in place, but his eyes danced with pleasure, and an air of electricity surrounded him. A calm before the storm sensation had goose bumps racing up her arms in anticipation.

"Good morning, Gabriella." His husky voice reached across the room like a caress, making all of her nerve endings stand up and say hello.

"Morning." She nodded with a polite smile, then went back to making breakfast.

Stop it, she told her shaking hands. *Your divorce isn't even final yet and already you're wondering how he kisses.*

"You're on breakfast duty already?" He set his black hat on the rack by the doorway.

"Kind of. Greta's not feeling well."

He looked at her sharply, his brows drawn down in a deep frown. "Is she all right?"

"She's a bit nauseated."

His breath eased out and he leaned against the counter. "I remember when she was pregnant with Luke, she had the worst morning sickness. Thankfully that only lasted a few weeks."

Greta emerged from the bathroom, drying her hand on her jeans.

"Hey Greta girl," Mark greeted. "Trey told me the good news. Congratulations."

"Are you sure?" she asked with a skip of hesitation.

The question made Gabriella pause mid-egg break. What did *that* mean?

"Yeah." He gave her a brief hug. "I'm happy for you."

"Really?" Her relief was palpable.

"Of course. You guys are the best parents I know. It's going to be fine."

"Thanks, Mark." She hugged him again. "I'm so glad you're back."

"Me too," he murmured into her hair.

Gabriella kept her focus on her task feeling decidedly un-comfortable, as if she were witnessing something she shouldn't. There was a definite vibe between the two of them that felt far too intimate for someone considered a friend, even a close family friend, and questions began to swirl through her brain. Mark had gone somewhere? Why? Why would Greta be concerned if he was happy about her pregnancy?

Nope. She mentally slammed the door on that train of thought. She had no business knowing anything about anyone. These people were strangers. Nice strangers, but strangers nonetheless and their history had absolutely nothing to with her.

"Oh, Gabriella," Greta exclaimed. "I didn't mean to make you do all of the work."

"That's okay. Here." She handed Greta the box of crackers.

"I found these. Why don't you go lie down or get some fresh air? I can take care of this."

"Are you sure?"

"No problem. Just tell me how many I'm cooking for."

"Eight, including you. I think I'll stick to the crackers." She grimaced as she looked fondly at the mound of sausages lying on a platter in all of their caramel dark deliciousness.

"Are they as big as him?" She nodded at Mark.

Greta smiled. "Some are bigger."

"I'll break more eggs."

"Thanks again. I'll owe you. See ya, Mark." With crackers in hand, she left them on their own.

Mark reached for a mug and poured himself some coffee. "How are you doing?"

"Fine," she replied before he finished asking the question.

"Gabriella." The sharp crack in his tone made her gaze jump to his. "Really, how are you doing?" The set of his jaw and the earnest worry in his eyes told her that he wanted an honest answer and that it mattered to him.

She turned away from the temptation of leaning her head against that strong chest and poured the eggs onto the hot skillet. The bubbling yellow mixture was an excellent representation of how Mark's gaze set her insides to quivering. "I don't know. I'm standing. My body doesn't ache. I have no clue what I am going to do, or where I'll live, or how I'll make any money. But I'm alive. That's the most important thing. Right?"

"That's a start. One step at a time. I have a feeling you're going to be just fine." There was a softness in his gaze that made her heart beat in triple time. "Gabriella—" he began then was interrupted by the pounding of heavy footfalls coming through the mudroom.

She almost dropped the hot pan in her hand as she watched

the parade of fine male specimens coming through the door. They not only varied in height from tall to gigantic, but also in hair color and ages. Each was handsome in their own way, and so supremely virile her throat went dry just by being in their presence. No wonder Greta was pregnant. Just being around so much testosterone.

"Dear Lord. I must be dreaming." A smooth baritone interrupted her shameless ogling.

Glancing over, she saw a devil in the flesh staring at her like she was filet mignon at an all you could eat buffet. He stood a foot shorter than Mark and had a lean wiry build like the bull riders she used to follow as a kid. His sandy blond hair was short in the back, longer in the front, with his bangs hanging down in front of his laughing blue eyes. Stubble covered his cheeks and surrounded a wide easy grin. He looked as if he just rolled out of bed after a very enjoyable sleepless night.

Despite her seconds-old promise to stay cool and unaffected, she found herself answering his smile with one of her own.

"Hi. I'm Jack Cannon." He reached across Mark, who stood between them, leaning against the counter, and offered her his hand.

"Gabriella Montoya." The kiss he placed on the back of her hand tingled but didn't send her senses into overdrive the way that simply looking at Mark did. Interesting.

"Montoya?" Jack raised his brow and looked back at a very annoyed Rafe. "Any relation to you?"

"She's my sister and let go of her hand."

"Excellent." He turned back to her and turned up the wattage on his smile. "For a second I thought you might be a relative of Greta's. You kinda look alike. Why aren't you staying at our place? There's plenty of space for you with us."

"Lay off, Cannon," Rafe growled.

The sound made his eyes burn brighter with an inner laughter. "How long do we have the pleasure of your company, Gabriella?" He drawled her name out.

"I'm not sure yet. Hopefully, not too long. I wouldn't want to overstay my welcome."

"As if that's a possibility." He looped his thumbs into his belt. "Is this your first visit to Mission?"

"Yes." There was a playfulness about him that had her giggling in the wake of his saccharine charm. Her bullshit meter was going off the charts, but she sensed his flirtatious nature was so ingrained in his DNA, he'd try to charm the stripes off a zebra.

"I would be more than happy to show you around. Give you the VIP tour." He took a step closer and was stopped by Mark's black boot.

"I'd back off there, Jack, before Rafe breaks you in two," he murmured quietly.

Mr. Dark and Dangerous was back, with a ramrod-stiff posture that at first glance was deceptively casual. The muscles of his face were relaxed, as if he was simply enjoying a cup of piping hot coffee, but his eyes glowed with an intensity that had all of the trembles she hadn't felt with Jack's handshake erupting over her body.

For some reason, his softly spoken warning made Jack happier. "Just let me know if you want that tour." He winked, then sat down with the other men.

"Can I carry anything for you?" Mark asked in that same low tone.

Her tongue seemed to be stuck to the roof of her mouth, and it took a few seconds before she could answer. "Sure."

His long fingers covered her hand as she handed him a platter. Her heart jumped in her throat as her gaze flew to his face. He stared down at her, his lips parted slightly. She swallowed hard. Part of her wanted to drop the platter and kiss him to see if his lips were as firm as they looked. The other part of her wanted to drop the platter and run the other way with some semblance of self-preservation.

The excited yip of a dog preceded Trey as he entered the kitchen and broke the spell. "Good morning, gentlemen."

Daisy, the Australian shepherd Greta introduced to her the night before, circled her legs twice before sitting at her feet to stare at the platter of sausages, tongue lolling out of her mouth. When neither of them made a move, she yipped again and nudged Mark's leg with her nose.

"Daisy, you know better than to beg," Mark said even as he tossed the dog a bit of meat. "She's still new and learning," he explained. "I guess we're all learning our limits with each other."

"Uh-huh." Gabriella turned to resume her task as she sucked in a steadying breath. She prayed her hands would stop shaking long enough to get the food to the table without dropping anything.

"I just checked on Greta," Trey said when she placed a plate in front of him. "Thanks for the help this morning, Gabriella. We both appreciate it."

"It's the least I could do for you for letting me say here." She took the seat to his right. "How is she doing?"

"Better. Hopefully she'll be back down in a few. Have you met everyone yet?"

"Just Mark and Jack."

"Well, let's change that." Trey made the rounds of introductions, and soon the men fell into easy conversation about what needed to be done around the ranch.

"Where is Greta?" Colby asked around a mouthful of eggs.

"She's resting. Morning sickness is getting to her." Trey smiled behind his mug.

All movement stopped. The sudden stillness even made Gabriella pause, her fork hovering at her lips.

"Get out!" Adam exclaimed.

As one, every man hopped up with shouts of congratulations and backslapping. Trey's smile was wide, but Gabriella could see the strain in his eyes. Now that she knew their history, she saw how worried he was for his wife and child.

While the group resettled in their seats, she thought about her own situation. She was not alone in the shitty-things-happened-to-good-people department. At least in her case, a child had not been affected by the ugliness her marriage had become. With the Armstrongs, she was reminded of one elemental truth: however bad you think your life is, there is always someone, somewhere having a worst time of it. What defined a person was how they turned that tragedy into triumph.

As she ate her breakfast, she looked around and mentally shook her head. Here she was, surrounded by big, burly men who could knock her across the room without a second thought if they wanted. After what she had gone through, this should be the last place she should feel comfortable, even safe, but she found them quite fascinating to watch. Everyone was treated with the same respect and courtesy, no matter their age or time spent on the ranch.

Having spent the last few years with people who judged her by the cut of her clothes and the make of her car, these men were a breath of Aramis-free air. To think, she had actually busted her ass to be accepted in that lifestyle. When had she become so shallow?

"What are your plans for today, Lita?" Rafe's quiet question broke into her maudlin thoughts.

She shrugged. "I'm not sure. Part of me wants to crawl back into bed for a long as possible, but I think I'll go into town and do some shopping. Get clothes that are a little more suited to the ranch." She gestured at the cashmere sweater and black slacks she wore.

"Do you want me to take you?"

"No, no." She waved away his offer. "I'll do fine on my own."

He just nodded with a wary squint to his eyes. He didn't appear confident about leaving her to her own devices. He looped his arm around her shoulder. "I've missed you, Lita. I'm glad you're here."

"Me too." She blinked back the tears and hugged him tight. There had been so few opportunities to see him during her marriage, and she truly missed her big, bothersome brother.

"I'll meet up with you guys later." Trey took one last sip of coffee before setting his mug in the dishwasher. "I want to check on Greta first."

Mark was the last to leave. He pulled a slip of paper from his pocket and handed it to her. "Here's a list of all of our cell numbers. If you need anything, don't hesitate to call any of us."

The paper was still warm from his body heat. She cradled the paper close to her breast, touched by his thoughtfulness. "Thank you."

He nodded then set his hat on his head, tilting it low on his forehead. His dark eyes met hers and the corner of his mouth lifted up. "I'll be seeing you." He turned on his heel and walked away.

Her gaze stayed glued to his denim covered-ass until he was gone.

"I'm in so much trouble," she whispered to the empty room.

Chapter Six

"HEY, MARK, RAFE. Can you come here?" Ben called from across the yard, then disappeared into the barn.

The two men shared a frown and walked into the shadowy interior where they were met with four very grim and sober faces.

"Who are we on the lookout for?" Ben asked, cutting right to the chase.

Mark studied each silent figure and saw in their set jaws that every man understood the seriousness of the situation. "Ex-husband," he replied. "What can you tell us about him, Rafe?"

"His name is Drew Daws. Blond, not much taller than me. He wears fancy suits and designer labels. He's a lawyer, something to do with real estate. I never understood what he was talking about. Lita met him at the country club she was working at. God." He kicked the sawdust on the floor. "I should have known he was a rat-ass bastard."

"I take it you didn't like him," Mark said, stating the obvious.

"No brother likes the man his sister is sleeping with. But this guy…" He shook his head. "He was too slick. Too into material things. I didn't think Lita could handle him. I don't mean handle, but we grew up on an apple orchard in Yakima. This was a man who spent ten grand on a watch because he liked the shine. I was afraid she'd get swallowed up in all of that. But she seemed happy, she had financial security, so I didn't say anything. I should have. Maybe if I had—"

"She would have been pissed at you." Mark saw the self-loathing and guilt stamped on Rafe's face. Trey had that look once. It came from feeling like you couldn't protect the ones you loved. No matter how badly you wanted to. "From personal experience, I know there's nothing a woman hates more than having her choices questioned by her big brother. Makes them jump into more danger just to prove you wrong."

Rafe shook his head again. "I still should have known."

"Did you two keep in contact much?" Ben asked.

"Not a whole lot. They were married over two years ago. She lived in the city, I was traveling with the Jangula family and their equestrian show at the time. We talked every few months on the phone, sent emails. The last time I saw her was a few months after her wedding day. She was so happy then." He blinked hard, and Mark saw furious tears shining in his eyes.

"She's going to be all right, Rafe. She's a strong girl." He couldn't blame the guy for being upset. If anyone hurt Melody, he'd want their head on a spike.

Ben nodded. "Where's the ass now?"

"Awaiting trial," Mark answered. "He's out on bail now, but he has powerful friends on the loose."

Ben nodded again. "So we have what, two, three days before he tracks her down and tries to make contact?"

"Do you think he will?" Adam crossed his arms as his frown deepened.

Ben raised his brows. "Think about it. You are a man who places great value in your appearance and possessions, and your favorite toy has you up on charges for spousal abuse. What would you do?"

Silence descended upon them as they each considered the possibilities. Mark's flesh crawled at the thought of Gabriella being in even more danger. One by one, he met the eyes of each man. They all nodded once at him, determination on their faces.

Rafe slumped even more under the weight of his fear for his sister. Mark placed a hand on his shoulder. "She's safe here. None of us are going to let her get hurt. Right, guys?" He motioned to the others.

"Right," they all agreed in unison.

"Yeah." Rafe lifted his head. Revenge glittered in his brown eyes. "If I see him, I'll kill him."

Mark tightened his grip. "That's why we're going to watch your back, too."

"I can take care of myself."

"You're part of our family now. Keeping each other out of jail is what we do."

The faintest of smiles touched Rafe's lips. When the words wouldn't come, he nodded again.

"I'm willing to share my room with Gabriella," Jack chimed in. "That way we can keep an eye on her, 24/7."

"Jack," Mark and Rafe warned in unison in a low, menacing tone.

His smile grew larger. "It was just a suggestion."

The idea of anyone lying down with Gabriella had Mark seeing red. His nostrils flared before he reined in the emotion. "Let's get to work, men, and keep your eyes and ears open."

With that, he hustled out of the barn even as his palm itched to slap that smirk off Jack's face. Usually he found the man mildly entertaining, but today the teasing was beyond annoying.

With jerky hands he yanked a stick of gum from his front pocket. The snap of spearmint mixed with the pungent aroma of cows hit his nose as he marched into the corral. The noxious smell did its job and cleared his head.

What was he going to do about Gabriella? He wanted her, no question about that. Being in the same room with her, hell, just thinking about her, made his body ache in an all-too pleasurable way. He was so stiff he could barely walk straight, and no matter how much he shifted his growing erection, there was no willing it down.

She was just so lush, with all of that thick hair cascading over her shoulders. And her hourglass figure was so ripe, he could spend hours worshipping her, giving her every pleasure she desired.

God, what was wrong with him? He was lusting after a woman who was abused by a man she trusted. The last thing she needed was another man breathing down her neck, hoping for a little action of the sexy kind.

The snapping sound of his gum echoed in the corral as his brain worked out the conundrum. Would she even welcome his advances? The way she had looked at him when she thought he wasn't noticing had made him thankful for the cover of the breakfast table. Interest glowed in her dark gaze, but if he were ever to show her the full force of his desires, would she crumble and relive the worst moments of her marriage?

He shook his head. He wasn't giving her enough credit. The minute she realized just how much danger she was in, she had hightailed it out of that situation. She had the courage and bravery to do something about her abuse, to prevent it from happening again. Gabriella might have made the mistake of trusting the wrong person, but it was the ass's fault for abusing that trust. She was a fighter. She might have been beaten, but she was not broken.

He rubbed at the ache forming between his eyes. Things were getting complicated.

The image of Gabriella when he handed her the list of phone numbers came to mind. Her soft smile, the delighted surprise in her rich brown eyes. She was happy and he was the one who had given that to her. He wanted to do it again.

Yeah, he wanted to make her happy.

Okay. The girl wasn't leaving any time soon, and neither was his infatuation. The best course of action was probably to follow her lead. Let her know he was interested, but take his cues from her. Trey and Greta lived by one motto: "One day at a time." He could do that, too.

"Good morning, Mr. Mark." A short, round man greeted him from the door.

"Hey, Jorge, how's it going?"

"*Bueno*, thank you. Are the men ready?"

"Yeah." This time he couldn't hold back his sigh. "They're ready."

"*Excellente.* I'll get the equipment."

"Great."

Just his luck. Today of all days was the morning he had to supervise the masturbation of their bulls for their prized semen.

Could the day get any better?

Chapter Seven

"FEELING BETTER?" GABRIELLA asked Greta when she ventured back into the kitchen. She closed the latch on the dishwasher and set it to start.

"Much." Greta sighed. "I had forgotten how bad this part was. Last time it only lasted a month. I hope it's the same this go-round." She set the box of crackers down within reaching distance. "Thanks again. I really appreciate it."

Gabriella smiled. "Like I told Trey, it's the least I can do."

The other woman smiled back then reached into the cupboard and took down a mug. "So, what are your plans for today?" she asked over her shoulder as she filled the kettle with water and set it on the stove.

"I thought I would head into town and get a few things. I don't think my Jimmy Choos would appreciate the terrain around here."

"Jimmy Choos?" Greta gasped then sighed with a dreamy expression on her face. "Oh, I remember a time when I wore fancy shoes." She snorted in laughter. "I remember a time when I didn't use the word 'fancy.' When did I become such a hick?"

"But you love it here." There was no mistaking the contented look on Greta's face.

"I do. I never thought I'd be happy without the hustle and

bustle of city life. But the hands and my work keep me busy. A baby will just add to the craziness." She giggled. "I can't wait. Hey, I need to go to the post office. How about I drive you around? Give you a tour?"

"That would be nice, if you're feeling up to it."

"I'll be fine. It's odors that cause me the most trouble. If I get sick, I'll just gak on the side of the road. Worst things have happened out there."

Gabriella couldn't keep the horrified expression at bay. "Are you serious?"

Greta's laughter echoed in the empty kitchen. "You should see your face right now. Hey, you gotta do what you gotta do. Besides, you grew up in farm country, you should know better. I'll be okay. Really."

"It's been a long time since I've been on a farm. I guess you ranchers are more comfortable with nature." She smiled.

Thirty minutes later, they were trundling down the lane leading away from the ranch.

"So why does Rafe call you 'Lita'?" Greta asked as she turned onto the dusty two-lane road toward the small town of Mission.

"Well, you know that in most Spanish dialects you add 'ita' to a name and it means 'little.' So 'Gabrielita' is 'little Gabriella,' which is a mouthful. So after a while it just became 'Lita,' " she explained.

"So is Rafe 'Rafaelito'?"

"Not really." She laughed. "It doesn't quite roll off the tongue, and he was never really little. Rafe was the only nickname he'd tolerate."

"Yeah, these cattle boys are all big." Greta flashed a worried glance in her direction. "Does that bother you? Being around such large men?"

"No, but I understand why you think it would. I know not every man on the planet is out to hurt me, and I trust Rafe. If he thinks I'm safe here, then I'm safe."

"You do know that you just inherited six big brothers. They'll look out for you. Whether you want them to or not."

"Have they worked for you all a long time?"

"Well, Trey and Mark grew up together. Ben's been there for, gosh, over twenty years now. The rest came on in the last couple of years or so."

"They all seem nice." She grinned at the memory of one man in particular. "Jack's a flirt."

Greta rolled her eyes. "Oh, that boy. Both he and Adam can be more than a handful. But while they may appear like everything is a joke or a potential for a good time, when it comes time to get down to business, they're right there ready for you."

"Mark seems a bit…intense," she said, hoping Greta would take the lead and reveal some juicy details. There were so many things she wanted to know about that man.

"Mark," Greta sighed on a breath that sounded both wistful and full of regret. "When Trey was struggling with, well, everything, Mark was always there for me."

Gabriella waited to see if she'd say more. Moments later her patience paid off as Greta's gaze turned retrospective.

"There was a time when there might have been something more between us. Way back when. But I knew that those feelings were just my hurt pride talking." Greta pulled into a parking space. The tick of the cooling engine filled the small silence as Greta gazed into the distance. "I've always felt horrible about using Mark that way. Relying on him for so much. He's such a great guy, and any woman would be so fortunate to have him. God, you must think I'm so shallow."

"No, shallow is accepting diamond earrings after your husband slaps you."

"Oh God, Gabriella." She placed a hand on her arm. "Don't think about yourself in that way. You wanted to believe in someone you trusted. It was his fault he broke that trust. And you didn't let him buy you off a second time. You got out. That was so brave."

"It doesn't feel very brave." She shook her head then flashed a sheepish grin. "People do whatever they have to in order to feel better about themselves and the choices they make. I guess what's important is how you make things right when it matters most. Does Mark still have feelings for you?" She couldn't explain why Greta's answer mattered so much.

"No, he doesn't. He went away for a while, and when he came back he said that he had reconciled all of those emotions. Part of me was afraid he was just saying that so I wouldn't feel guilty." She paused and then looked up at Gabriella with a spark of clarity in her eyes. "But you know, I really think he's moved on."

"Which is good, right?"

"Yeah." A slow smile spread across her face. "I think it's going to be really good."

Not quite sure what the smile meant, Gabriella just nodded. "Well, great."

Greta shook her head and pushed the hair off her face. "I'm sorry I spilled all of that on you. It's not like I can talk to any of the guys about things like emotions and feelings, and my closest female friend is Mark's sister, Melody. It's not something I really wanted to discuss with her."

"I can imagine. Well, I'm glad I could help." And learn valuable information in the process. She looked out the window then frowned. "Why are we at the feed store?"

Greta laughed. "Believe it or not, this is the best place to find jeans around here."

"Seriously?"

"Yep."

She let out a long breath. "I am so going to stick out like a sore thumb around here."

"Only for a little bit. We can try to dim your sparkle. But I have to tell you, you're going to stick out anyway. You're so beautiful, nothing can diminish that."

Gabriella blinked. She had never been given a compliment like that from another woman without a biting cut down following. "Thank you. Although I think your maternal glow will outshine me."

Greta wrinkled her nose. "I knew I liked you. Come on. Let's countrify you."

Chapter Eight

G ABRIELLA PLOPPED DOWN on the front porch swing with
a tired sigh, the muscles in her legs and butt throbbing in
protest.

Greta's grand plan to have a big welcome dinner in Gabriella's honor went horribly awry when the scent of sweating onions
sent her into the bathroom for a long half hour, leaving
Gabriella to finish up the cooking for seven hungry men.

She hadn't worked so hard in years. Her fingers were pruny
and sweat made her blouse stick to the middle of her back, but
for the first time in forever she felt a sense of accomplishment.
Funny how cooking a simple meal meant more to her than
planning a dinner party for twenty of Drew's most important
clients. Maybe because she knew that this time, her efforts were
going to be appreciated and not nitpicked over every tiny detail.
Or perhaps it was because she knew this group of men had
worked their asses off all day and she hoped they enjoyed what
little she could provide.

With another sigh, she stuck out her denim-clad legs and
stared across the fields of drying grass. The sun was setting on
the opposite side of the house in brilliant shades of yellows and
pinks, leaving her in the soft purple pre-evening shadows.

"Care for some company?"

She bit her lip and tamped down the thrill of excitement that deep voice ignited within her belly. Shifting her gaze, her breath lodged in her throat at the sight of Mark standing at the bottom of the stairs. He looked so tall and masculine, with his black hat shielding his eyes and emphasizing the strong line of his jaw. Her lips tingled just thinking about brushing kisses along that firm line.

"Sure," she said and scooted over to give him more room beside her.

The swing jostled with his added weight, and he placed his hat on his lap as he practically melted into the corner, stretching his well-muscled arm along behind her. How nice would it feel to snuggle against that broad chest and get up close and personal with that manly scent?

She swallowed hard and shifted her gaze away from the temptation of his chambray-covered chest. "How was your day?"

The corner of his mouth quirked up and the skin around his eyes crinkled as if she said something funny. "Let's just say our bulls are real happy." Since she wasn't sure exactly what that meant, she just nodded in return.

"How was the shopping?" he asked.

"Good. Got some jeans and a pair of boots." He looked pointedly at her bare feet and raised his brow. She wiggled her pedicured toes. "I'm more comfortable without shoes."

"I'm glad you feel like you can be yourself, and that you feel comfortable enough to sit with me like this."

She frowned. "Why shouldn't I be?"

"We're alone, and I'm a strange man. It would make sense if you were a bit frightened."

"Are you planning on doing me harm?"

"Never." His jaw tightened. "I'd never hurt you, Gabriella."

The ferocity of his vow sent chills down her bare arms. "If I go around thinking every man I'm going to encounter is out to hurt me, then I will always live in fear. If I'm always afraid, then he wins. He will have taken my life away as surely as if he'd killed me. There's no way I'm going to let him win."

"You're very brave."

She shook her head. "Everyone keeps saying that. I'm not brave. I'm just trying to survive."

"Darlin', sometimes choosing to live in the face of adversity is the bravest choice one can make. I'm sure there are a lot of women who would have given up. You said you had enough and did something about it. That decision put you way ahead of the game."

Her first inclination was to dispute the praise she heard in his voice, but then she bit her tongue. She wanted a life, a good life. Nothing extravagant, but also no less than what she deserved. She had to stop apologizing for wanting something that should be a basic human right.

"Do you still love him?" he asked in a low voice.

"No," she answered immediately and turned her gaze back to the land. "No, I've thought a lot about it for some time now. When I was a kid, all I wanted was to get out of that shack of a farmhouse and go someplace that wasn't constantly covered in dust. I wanted to live in a house with shiny appliances and tile floor and more than one bathroom. When I met Drew, he was everything I ever wanted. Successful, good looking, wealthy. When he started to shower me with attention, I couldn't believe that he actually wanted the poor girl from the apple orchard. Once we were married, I was so happy and relieved to not have to worry about money anymore that I overlooked how he slowly cut me off from my friends. How he and his mother kept my days filled with women's club meetings and charity work that they took all of the credit for to further his image. I know I should have left him the first time he hit me, but I was so afraid of the unknown. After that, it just didn't matter anymore. I might have cared for him once, but I realized I never really loved him. I loved what he represented. Does that make any sense?"

He nodded with a small humorless smile. "I know exactly what you mean."

She thought about what Greta had told her earlier about her and Mark's past and curiosity prompted her to ask, "Have you ever been in love?"

His gaze flicked away and he leaned forward to rest his arms on his thighs. When he looked back at her he let out a long sigh. "I thought I was, once."

"What happened?" she asked when he didn't continue.

"Just like you, I realized I loved what she represented. Family, a partner, loyalty. She was the first woman I met who was everything I ever wanted." A rueful smile twitched across his lips and he leaned back. "Except she was in love with someone else. And they were perfect for each other. I harbored those feelings for much longer than I should have. Wasted a lot of years that I could have had for my own happiness. After I realized what I had done, I promised myself that when I found the woman for me, I'd never let her go."

"Do you think you'll find her?"

The heat that simmered in his obsidian gaze warmed her as if she stood in front of a bonfire. "I know I will."

Wow. Greta had been right. The woman who ended up with Mark would be a very lucky girl indeed.

It was easy for her to imagine what it would be like being held in his strong arms. To feel those big calloused hands stroking over her bare skin. Her breasts swelled under the weight of his gaze at the thought. Could he see her nipples pebble under her blouse?

Her own gaze trailed down his chest to the six-pack she knew lay beneath his shirt, She wanted to spend hours tracing each muscle with her tongue. Under the hat that lay on his lap, the muscles of his thighs bunched as he pushed the swing back and forth.

"Darlin', your eyes are making promises I don't think you can keep."

Her gaze flew to his face, and her heart pounded in her chest. A flush graced his cheeks and his full lips were soft and parted.

"What promises are those?" She didn't recognize the husky-voiced response as belonging to her.

"Long, slow, drugging kisses, full body contact, and scream-ing orgasms."

She blinked twice. "Funny. I wouldn't have taken you for a screamer."

The swing stopped. His head fell back as he let out a loud rumble of laughter. Gabriella watched with fascination as his whole body shook. Dimples creased both of his cheeks and begged her to kiss and lick the indentations.

"Did we miss the joke?" Rafe bounded up the stairs with Ben and Colby following behind.

Mark adjusted his hat to cover more of his lap. "Your sister's quite the firecracker." Behind her, he twisted a lock of her hair around his fingers and tugged it playfully.

"Oh yeah? What was so funny?"

She rolled her eyes at her brother. "I was telling him the story of when you were little and kept eating the apricots off the tree every time you passed by, and the way it affected your digestive system."

Colby and Ben snickered as Rafe's eyes narrowed with murderous intent. "You're so not funny, Lita."

She gave him a brilliant smile and a bat of her lashes. "I better check on dinner." She got to her feet then looked down at Mark. "I look forward to finishing that conversation."

"Me too," he said in a low murmur that confirmed what she hoped.

He was interested. *Yes!*

"What conversation would that be?" Rafe asked in all of his nosy glory.

"The best way to annoy big brothers. Now be nice to me or no enchiladas for you."

"*Abulita's* recipe?"

Her brows rose in disbelief that he had to ask. "Of course."

He hooted and rubbed his hands together before dashing into the house before her. Colby displayed more manners and held the screen door open for her.

"Coming, boss?" she heard Ben ask behind her. "I mean, are you following?"

"In a second," Mark replied with a low rumble.

"Is your hat moving on its own?"

"Shut up, Ben."

Chapter Nine

H OW COULD ONE man's gaze burn her like a blowtorch set on high?

During her marriage, the sexual chemistry had been good, but it was nothing like the excitement she felt sitting next to Mark at the dinner table. All of her senses were attuned to his every move, his every breath. From his scent of Old Spice and spearmint to his low rumbles of appreciation. The shifting of his thigh muscles alongside hers under the table brought to mind images of him thrusting inside her wet and achy sheath. The glances he flicked her way were hotter than the peppers on her tongue, and she lost track of how many glasses of water she drank in an attempt to cool the fire he lit within.

God, she hoped she responded correctly to the questions the others asked her during the meal. The last thing she needed was to come off as a complete goober, or worse, have Rafe start to suspect something was up.

"Ladies." Ben stood and gathered his dishes. "That was excellent. You sure know how to spoil us." The rest of the men nodded.

Mark stopped her as she began to stack the dishes. "There's a rule around here. Whoever cooks dinner gets to relax while the others clean up."

"Yeah," Greta chimed in. "I usually sit on the swing with a glass of wine. Why don't you join me? You can have the wine, I'll make do with grape juice."

"All right. But I can at least help clear the table." She collected a few utensils and then her plate.

When she stood, Mark's big hand covered hers, just like it had that morning. In the back of her mind, she was vaguely aware that the others had gone into the kitchen and they were all alone in the dining room. Her gaze lifted to his face and her lips parted as she saw the desire in his eyes. A second later his mouth was on hers, hot and firm. She barely registered the texture of his lips when he pulled away and disappeared without a sound into the kitchen.

Shock held her immobile for several long seconds before her tongue swept her lower lip in an attempt to recapture his flavor. *What the hell?*

What just happened? That was the briefest kiss she ever had in her life, yet it ignited a fire within that she feared could only be quenched with his cock buried deep within her body. Holy hell, she wasn't prepared to fall so hard so fast. This was bad. This was very bad.

"Gabriella, are you okay?" Greta asked from the doorway.

"What?" She spun around. "Sure. Fine."

"Here." Greta handed her a glass of wine. "Hopefully it's not too cold outside to enjoy the swing."

Gabriella followed, but her mind was still on that kiss. She settled onto the side of the glider seat Mark occupied earlier that evening and looked out into the black horizon. The abrupt change her life had taken the last few days was making her head reel.

Perspective. She had to put it all into perspective.

Okay, girl, use your head.

Here was a man she'd known for all of one day. Physical attraction was brief and immediate, everyone knew that, so to find the man desirable wasn't completely out of the scope of reality. The question was what to do with all of this newly discovered lust. Mark did not appear like a one-night stand kind of guy, but she really didn't have anything else to offer with her life in limbo until the trial was over and done with. Besides, wasn't she supposed to be having some kind of post-matrimonial, grieving, cooling-off period? Wasn't she supposed to be numb from the waist down for at least six months, if not longer? Maybe she was a slut, just like Drew said.

"Care to talk about it?"

"What?" She turned her head to see Greta watching her with a furrow in her brow. "Talk about what?"

"Whatever it is that has your brain working so hard."

"Oh, it's nothing." She took a sip of wine. The rich spice of the syrah coated her tongue and reminded her of kissing Mark.

"Is it your ex?"

She couldn't stop the bark of laughter that erupted. "No, definitely not thinking about my ex."

"Is it Mark, then?"

Her heart stopped as she sputtered into her glass. "What? Why would you think that?"

Greta rolled her eyes. "Oh, please. I was sitting across from you at dinner. I've never seen two people be more aware of each other while trying their hardest not to be. There was so much electricity between you two, I could feel it. It was so hot. I was half tempted to drag Trey off to our room to have my wicked way with him."

"Oh my God." Was she so transparent? "Did everyone notice?"

"No, they're men. Besides, I'm sure you would have heard

about it if Rafe suspected you had a thing for his boss."

Gabriella's shoulders sagged with relief. "I suppose so. Truthfully, I don't know what I'm thinking. I'm just so confused."

"Well, what are you confused about?"

She laughed. "Don't you think it's poor form to be mid-divorce and already harboring illicit thoughts about another man?"

"That's the funny thing about life, Gabriella, it's not black and white. Do you still have feelings for your ex-husband?"

She chuckled again. "If you mean positive ones, no."

Greta nodded as if she already suspected that answer. "Did you come to that conclusion before or after you met Mark?"

"Before."

Nodding again, she looked out into the distance. "Sometimes we're so worried about doing what's considered appropriate that we miss out on doing what's right. When Trey lost his memory a few months ago, we sat right here on his first night back from the hospital. Talk about feeling confused. It was the first time in forever that he talked to me, spent real time with me, and I missed him so much. The Trey I knew and loved was back. He couldn't remember the bad times we had, so it was as if we were starting all over. All I wanted to do was hold him and kiss him, but for all intents and purposes he'd only known me one day. I didn't think it was appropriate to throw myself at him, and at the same time he didn't want to pressure me when his head was still messed up. So because of propriety we waited before we took that next intimate step."

"How long did you wait for?"

"Twenty-four long hours." She smiled and shyly batted her lashes, but Gabrielle sensed she wasn't the least bit apologetic. "Look, if there is one thing I learned through Luke's death and

Trey's accident, it's this. Life is short. You never know what's going to happen. You could have been killed that night, but you survived. You were given a second chance. Don't rush into danger, but at the same time don't be afraid to take risks. Do you pass up on happiness because a stranger may say it's not proper? Who cares? And Mark is a good man, a great man. The only people you should worry about are you and him. That's all that really matters."

Gabriella bit her lip and processed Greta's words. The woman did have a point. For the last few years, she had lived by what others thought and expected from her and almost wound up dead. Maybe it was past time to worry only about what she thought.

The screen door creaked open. Trey's blond head stuck out. "Hey, magpie, we're done in here. How do you feel about sitting next to me while I watch the game?"

"Will you hold me close?"

A long slow smile curled his lips. "As close as possible."

"How can I say no to that?" Greta got to her feet. "Are you coming, Gabriella? They all pig pile in the living room to watch the Mariners play."

"Maybe." She stood and followed while ruminating on Greta's words.

In the living room, the big-screen TV blared while the ranch hands splayed out on the leather couches or on the floor as if their bones had liquefied wherever they landed. All of that testosterone in one location, and at the center of them all was a dark-haired man who roped a lariat around her libido by simply breathing. There was no way she would be able to be in the same room as Mark without wanting to touch or stare at him the entire night like a lovesick school girl. How embarrassing.

"Hey, Gabriella. Why don't you sit next to me?" Jack asked,

patting the seat beside him.

"Actually, I think I'll just head upstairs. It's been a long day." She softened her refusal with a smile.

"Sweet dreams, then." He waggled his brows and flashed that rakish grin.

Mark caught her gaze when she turned to leave. Those dark eyes stared straight into her soul. "Good night," he mouthed.

"Good night," she whispered back before racing up the stairs.

In the quiet of her room, her breathing sounded as ragged as a hyperventilating phantom. Her reflection in the mirror above the dresser showed a woman with bright, sparkly eyes, a becoming flush on her cheeks, and plump lips that appeared ready to be kissed good and hard. She looked alive.

"Well hello there," she said aloud. "I never thought I'd see you again."

The woman in the mirror smiled with a hint of naughty curling her lips.

Could she do this? *Should* she do this?

"Who controls your happiness?" the woman in the mirror asked.

Who controls your happiness?

Right.

Without another thought, she crossed to the dresser and picked up her hairbrush. It was time to claim a little piece of happiness for herself, even if just for one night.

It was time to catch a cowboy.

Chapter Ten

THE CRISP FALL air did nothing to cool Mark's blood as he made the trek from the main house back to his home. God, he was an idiot. He just had to go and see if Gabriella's lips were as soft as they looked, which of course they were. Softer, even. Now, that knowledge fueled his desire for another taste. A longer taste. A more dangerous taste.

Shoot, anyone could've walked in on them, but after the way his need for her had simmered all through that excruciatingly long dinner, he finally decided to damn the risk and satisfy his curiosity. Fat lot of good that did him.

He reached into his front pockets and came up empty. The back pockets and the one on his shirt were empty as well. Damn it. Who did he have to fuck to get a piece of gum?

Ugh, bad choice of words.

He slapped at all his pockets in a desperate search for at least one hidden stick of spearmint. No way was he going to break into his secret pack of Marlboros because he was horny. Those babies were for emergency use only.

"Are you all right?"

The soft question stopped him dead in his tracks. Holy shit, he was losing his mind. That, or he'd been kicked once too many times by a heifer. Hearing voices was not a sign of mental stability.

"Mark?" A shadow shifted on his front porch. "Are you okay?"

He squinted into the dark and recognized Gabriella's shape leaning against the porch railing. So he wasn't hallucinating. Wait a minute. Why was Gabriella waiting on his porch? In the dark? Alone.

"Mark?" she asked again and came down the first step. She had exchanged her blouse for a plush-looking sweater that hugged her curves in all of the right places. Damn, a man could get lost in all of that creamy cleavage. "Mark?"

"Wha-what?" He shook his head. "Um—I." Oh, right. "No. I'm fine. I gave up smoking not too long ago and still find myself reaching for a pack. Usually I have gum on hand, but I seem to be out."

"I've heard oral fixations can be tough to break." The moonlight caught the curve of her smile.

"Yeah." Sweet baby Jesus. "So, Gabriella. What brings you by?"

"Well, I—" The sound of Adam's boisterous laughter came down the road, followed by the murmurings of Rafe and Jack as they made their way back to the bunk house. "Could we take this conversation inside? Like now?"

"Sure thing." He swept past her, inhaling the subtle, musky scent of her perfume as he opened the door and gestured for her to enter first. "I take it Rafe doesn't know you're here?"

"Do you want Rafe to know I'm here?"

"No."

She laughed. "I thought so."

A lone floor lamp illuminated the entryway, casting a romantic glow over his rather worn and minimalist living room furniture. The amber light caressed Gabriella, making her look like an angel standing before him. An angel on a mission, he'd guess if the determined set of her jaw was any indication, and he had a feeling he knew what the purpose was for her visit.

"Why did you kiss me?" she asked the second he shut the door behind him.

Yep. He was right.

Now, what would be the best way to answer without him getting him decked for saying something inappropriate? Really, he had no right touching her in any way, shape, or form. If anything, he should apologize for being so forward.

But one look at her face decided his answer. "Because you're the most beautiful woman I've ever seen."

Her lips fluttered into a brief smile before they pressed into a thin line. "Is that the only reason?"

"No. It's because," he blew out a breath, "because I like you. A lot."

Several tense moments passed, and with each second the frown on her forehead deepened. "That's all? You think I'm pretty and you like me. That's it?"

"Yes. No. It's—I..." He blew out another breath and ran his hand through his hair. "I—I couldn't go another second without feeling your lips against mine. Okay? I know it was wrong. I'm sorry."

Her shoulders lowered, and a delighted smile replaced her frown. "The only wrong about that kiss was that it was over far too quickly."

"And happened far too soon. I shouldn't have invaded your personal space that way. Again, I'm sorry."

She shifted and took a step toward him. "Thank you for your apology. I greatly appreciate it." She took another step closer, boxing him between the door and her body. "I have a confession to make, Mark. I like you too. A lot."

"Yeah?" The smolder in her gaze felt as if it raised the temperature of the room at least another twenty degrees and turned the floor beneath him to quicksand, pulling him under fast. "Is that such a good idea?"

She let out a little laugh. "Now that's the question I've been asking myself all day. But you know, I'm tired of doing what I'm supposed to. It's time for me to do what I want."

He swallowed against the lump in his throat and suppressed a shiver when she pressed her breasts against his chest. "And what's that?"

"I want to kiss you."

Well hell, why didn't she just strip down to bare skin and throw herself in his arms. The effect on his senses would've been the same. "Ah, Gabriella, you are far too tempting. I don't want to take advantage of you."

"Who says you're taking advantage of me?" She planted her hands onto her hips and he saw a hint of the Latin fire that burned within. "I came here knowing full well what might happen."

"And what might that be?" he asked, his throat tight. His fingers clenched at his sides to keep from reaching out for her.

That siren's smile winked at him again. "Whatever we want. However we want. And as many times as we want."

He closed his eyes. "Jesus, Gabriella."

"Kiss me, Mark." Her hands came up to grip the sides of his waist. The heat of her palms burned him through his shirt. "Pretend that we're in the dining room back at the house and we're all alone. Kiss me like you wanted to kiss me."

"Fuck, baby girl," he moaned and gathered her closer. He didn't think twice and sealed his mouth over hers, parting her lips with a single thrust of his tongue. Forcing her to take all of him.

She tasted of red wine and cinnamon, a combination that reminded him of ambrosia. Sinful, decadent, and fit only for the gods. With a deep sigh, she twined her arms around his neck, knocking his hat to the floor as she tunneled her fingers through his hair and massaged his scalp.

Then she went and pressed her soft curves into his hard planes and blew his restraint all to hell. Her belly was the perfect cushion for his hard erection and with every move of her hips, pushed him further over the edge and sparking red lights to flash behind his closed eyelids.

His heart pounded hard behind his ribs, pushing all of his blood down to his groin. His fingers bit into the flesh of her hips with bruising force, making her whimper. The sound jolted him, forcing him to tear his mouth away and bury his face into the crook of her neck. He swept his hands up and down her back as he wrestled with his control.

"God, Gabriella, you drive me crazy." He drew in a deep breath and her designer perfume fragrance filled his lungs. Damn, why did she have to smell so good? All it did was make him want to eat her up.

"I want you to be crazy." She scraped her teeth along the stubble covering his jaw.

"No, no." He pushed her back an arm's distance away. With the door at his back, he was trapped between escape and temptation. "I'm too close to the edge. I don't want to hurt you by asking you for more than you're willing to give."

The warning in his growl made her freeze. She gazed up at him with shimmering deep brown eyes and her lips swollen and damp from his kisses. It took everything within him not to throw her on the floor and take her like a beast.

"Why do you think you'll hurt me?" she asked in a low, husky voice that was like a velvet glove to his senses.

He had to swallow twice before he could answer. "You're so tiny. Look how much taller I am than you. I want you so badly, Gabriella. I don't want to lose my control and do or say something that makes you think about—think about the bad things that have happened to you."

As he spoke, she lifted her hands and feathered her fingertips along his hairline. The light touch slowed his racing heart. He loosened his grip on her arms to allow her to press her weight against him. "I don't want you to fear me."

"Oh, Mark." She melted in his embrace. "By the sheer fact alone that you're worried you'll hurt me tells me that you won't." She stood up on tiptoe to nuzzle her nose under his chin like a kitten.

"I don't want to risk scaring you."

"And I don't want you to hold back. I want all of you."

"You say that now, but what happens when I'm on top of you, inside you, and all you see is *him*?"

She pulled back as if he'd stung her and the desire in her eyes shifted into fear. But it wasn't the type of fear that concerned him. The crease in her brow and the anxiety in her eyes appeared to be directed toward the woman within.

"Don't you think I worry about that too? That for the rest of my life I'll carry that fear and have that knee-jerk reaction to shy away from people? I can't live that way. I can't let him win." She ran her palms up and down the center of his chest. He wasn't certain if the gesture was to soothe him or her. "I'm not with you to spite him or to prove something to myself. I'm here because I like you. You make me feel…" she paused to chuckle. "You make me *feel*. I don't want to miss out on whatever this is because I'm afraid to move on. But I'm not going to force myself on you. If you want me to go, I'll go. If you want me, tell me. The truth. Do you want me, Mark?"

Slowly, gently, he lifted his hand and cupped her smooth cheek. She felt so delicate against his rough palm as he stroked her skin with his thumb. "I want you. More than anything."

A little breath eased past her lips as she nodded. Her eyes darted around the room and when her gaze landed on his cowboy hat at their feet she looked back to him with a raised brow. "Do you trust me?"

The question threw him. "What do you mean?"

"Do you trust me not to hurt you?"

Li'l Bit hurting him? The idea was almost laughable. "Darlin', you hurting me is not a concern of mine."

A wicked light entered her eyes and jump-started his heart rate. "Let me make sure I have this straight. You're worried that you want me so much, you'll lose control and hurt me, or do something to remind me of my ex-husband?"

"That's right."

"What if I were to tie you up?"

The words were slow to penetrate his thick skull, and even then he found it difficult to comprehend. Was this little angel of a woman suggesting something kinky?

"What?"

With a curl of her lips, her smile turned from angelic to devilish as he blinked at her with surprise and confusion. "If you're tied to the bed, then I would be responsible for how hard I push you. You won't have to worry about losing control because you won't be able to touch me. Can you do that, Mark? Can you give me the control and allow me to give us what we both want?"

The thought of being tied down and at her mercy made his knees buckle. When it came to sex, he was a pretty straightforward kind of guy—him in charge and his woman screaming his name in satisfaction in whatever position he pleased. That wasn't to say he was completely vanilla. He'd dabbled in a bit of bondage in the past, but he had been the one doing the tying.

But what Gabriella was suggesting was mighty-mighty interesting. Let her set the pace. Leave her with the option of when to pull back and when to push forward. And all he had to do was lie there and enjoy the ride.

What's your answer, cowboy?

"Yes."

By the way she lit it up, it was as if he had handed her the world. Her breath quickened and she practically danced on the balls of her feet. "Thank you. Now, show me to your room. Please," she added and held out her hand.

Chapter Eleven

G ABRIELLA COULDN'T BELIEVE the level of excitement that coursed through her blood. Simply knowing that this tough cowboy was going to give her full-on, unlimited access to his big, muscley body made her tremble. More than tremble, actually. Her teeth were doing a right-dead impersonation of a woodpecker at the moment. She'd have to be careful not to bite her tongue.

Sexual experimentation was not a new concept for her, and she would have been stunned if Mark had confessed that this was his first rodeo, but she sensed that playing a more submissive role was not the norm in his repertoire. No, he struck her as being large and in charge in the bedroom, which was probably why he feared for her safety. The sentiment was sweet and not entirely unwelcomed. Hearing him voice his concern convinced her she was right where she was supposed to be.

The heavy tread of his boots up the stairs matched the pounding of her heart. At the top of the landing, she discovered the top floor was one open space for the bedroom with a doorway to the right appearing to lead to the bath. The sight of his oversized wrought iron bed turned her legs to jelly. This was really going to happen. *Dear Lord, please don't let me hyperventilate.* Passing out from excitement wasn't the least bit sexy.

Mark turned on a lamp on the nightstand. "Hope you don't mind. I want to make sure you see exactly who it is you're making love to."

"Oh, sweetie, as if I could mistake you for anyone else." She rubbed her damp palms against her jeans. "So...do you have a rope handy?"

He laughed. "I love my work, but I don't bring it into the house. Let me think. Oh, I know." He went into the closest and pulled out two neckties. "Melody keeps buying me ties. She thinks it's funny trying to pretty me up." His wicked chuckle made her skin pebble. "She'd die if she knew what we're using them for."

"Very nice," Gabriella said as she took the fabric between her fingers and ran her thumb across the silk. She then draped them across the end of the bed and stepped right into his personal space. "From now on you have to do everything I say. Are you ready?"

His mouth opened, and he chuffed out a breath. He tried to speak again, but then snapped his teeth together and nodded.

Oh, this was going to be so good.

She lifted his right hand and placed a kiss at the center of his palm before undoing the button of his cuff. She did the same to his left hand then went to work on the fastenings of his shirt. Inch by slow inch the firm muscles of his chest were exposed and an ache began in her jaws, eager to sink her teeth into his pectorals. She pushed the shirt off his shoulders then reached for the hem of his undershirt and made quick work of pulling it up and over his head. Once he was bare, she stared unabashedly at the wide width of his torso that was smooth save for the patch of hair right in the center. The dusting trailed down his belly and circled his navel before disappearing into the band of his black jeans.

"Gabriella."

Mark's rough growl made her head jerk up. His black eyes glittered as his nostrils flared. "You're killing me, baby."

Giddy laughter tickled her lips, but she squashed the reaction. And to think, she hadn't really touched him yet.

"Lay down and stretch your arms up."

Holy cow, the man is a god, she thought as her blood heated while he stretched out on the mattress. Again, the urge to laugh bubbled up inside. How did she get so lucky?

She climbed onto the bed by his side and began to bind one of his wrists to the bars of the headboard. His skin was just as silky as the tie, but the fabric was much cooler in her hot hands. Leaning across him, she bound the other wrist, making sure to press her breasts against his face and wiggle a bit as she worked. The shifting of his hips and hot breaths into the cashmere delighted her to no end. Once finished, she tugged on the ties. "How's that? Too tight?"

"Nope. It's all good, darlin'." His long, slow smile launched the butterflies in her belly, and those amazing dimples winked at her as he settled deeper into the mattress. "But go ahead and test them again."

"Is that the game you want to play?" she said, laughing as she leaned forward to smother him with her breasts again before standing to move to the foot of the bed to tackle his boots. With one hand on the heel and the other around his ankle—well, mostly around his ankle—she tugged and grunted, succeeding only in breaking into a sweat. Gritting her teeth, she pulled again and the boot slid free with a *pop* and sent her flying back to land on her butt with a loud, "Umppf!"

"Are you okay?" Mark asked between fits of laughter.

She pushed her hair out of her eyes and stood. "I wouldn't be laughing, pretty boy."

"Sorry, but that was pretty damn funny."

"Ha ha." She gripped the second boot and pulled, slipping it off in one try. "See. I got this."

She removed his socks then crawled between his legs to sit on her knees and look down at her prize. With the tip of her finger, she traced a circle around his belt buckle, chuckling when he sucked in a hard breath.

"Still feel like laughing?" she asked as she scratched though the denim to the ridge beneath the fabric. The hard length jumped at her touch. "Ah, poor thing must be choking," she cooed and pulled down the zipper. Of course, black underwear.

Outlined through the cotton flared the generous head and long, thick stalk of his erection. The time for joking around was done as her mouth watered, hungering for a taste of the deep pink column. By the way she stripped his jeans and briefs off his legs, one would have thought it was Christmas morning and he was wrapped in Tiffany blue.

"God, Gabriella. I love the way you look at me," he rasped. "Your eyes are all glassy and your lips are parted like you can already taste me. You're burning me up."

Oh, she was just getting started. Like a spider, she crawled up her trapped prey, pressing her cashmere-covered breasts against the hard planes of his body as she revealed in his tortured hisses. Between her thighs, her pussy ached and she knew she was already wet and ready for him. Part of her wanted to get right down to business and ride him like a bull, but it'd be a tragedy to waste such a glorious opportunity.

She bent to trace the line of his abs with the tip of her tongue, stopping now and again to scrape her teeth against his bumps and ridges while he writhed helplessly beneath her.

"I want to see you," he panted. "I want to see you naked."

"Hey, who's in charge here?" She pulled away with a grin.

She grasped the hem of her sweater and lifted. "But since you asked so nicely."

Up and over her head went the sweater to flutter to the floor. She wiggled her jeans and panties off next, and with each item of clothing shed, his breath bellowed faster. He narrowed his eyes and his thick lashes made it appear as if he had coal lined around his eyes, giving him a dangerous, rock star appearance. That hint of restrained danger made her nipples tighten against the lace of her bra.

She loved the way his cock bobbed and his muscles flexed as she slowly lowered the right strap of her bra. The other strap she slipped down just as slowly before undoing the clasp in the back and removing the lace with an extra shimmy of her shoulders. Cupping her heavy breasts in her hands, she crawled back up his body, tugging on the dusky peaks of her nipples.

"You are so fucking beautiful." The reedy husk of his voice made her pussy gush more. Everything about the man was such a turn on.

The moment their bodies touched, she swore she heard their flesh sizzle with the heat they generated. He reared up and claimed her mouth in a hungry, desperate kiss that overwhelmed her senses. He bit her lips and thrust his tongue deep as if trying to make up for his inability to touch her.

Her lungs heaved and her lips throbbed when she pulled away. While she loved his kisses, she was hungry to explore the rest of him, but where oh where to begin? The bulge of his biceps was firm under her searching fingers, which she also discovered was a ticklish area as well as the line of his oblique, and if she dug the heel of her hands into his quadriceps, his toes curled in the most adorable fashion.

By the time she finally gripped him firmly by the base of his erection and cupped his balls, his skin was slick with sweat. He groaned so deeply, she felt the vibration in her hands.

She gently tugged on the hairs surrounding his cock and delighted in the answering growl. "You're not one for manscaping, I see."

"That's for. City boys," he gritted out between clenched teeth.

"Maybe I can ease you into it slowly. That way you can really feel it when I do this."

She flicked out her tongue to lick the sensitive skin of his balls. Around and around she licked and kissed the firm orbs. She worked her tongue up the long length and caught his gaze. With his feverish gaze focused firmly on her, she engulfed the crown of his cock and slurped as far down the shaft as she could fit into her mouth. He tasted so good all over, she could gladly dine on him for hours. Both hands joined in on the effort to make him lose his mind, and by the way he bucked and howled beneath her, she was doing a damn fine job. For a man who was the textbook definition of strong and silent, he sure was vocal. The power she held over him was so intoxicating, an inner strength flowed through her veins, making her feel like a super woman.

He was completely hers, powerless to stop her from pushing the utmost pleasure upon his senses, from taking him to the edge of oblivion and snatching him back at the last second. This big, strong, constantly in control man, who could break her with his bare hands, was pleading with her, begging her to finish the end of his torturous climb of pleasure. The knowledge shot straight to her core.

Mark's gorgeous eyes were glassy and unfocused as he stared down at her. "Please," he choked out. "Please."

She sat up and licked at the pre-cum leaking out of his shaft then slicked her thumb over the top, delighting in the way it throbbed in response. "Please, what?"

"Please," he panted and threw his head back with a painful howl. "God, baby, please, fuck me, please."

He was ready. He was more than ready.

"Where do you keep the condoms?" she asked.

"I don't know," he moaned, delirious. "Over. Somewhere. Please."

She would have laughed at his inability to form a sentence, except it was so damn sexy, she was near to mindlessness herself.

The logical choice was the nightstand. She yanked hard at the pull, dragging the entire drawer out of its slot and scattering the contents all over the floor. Foil packets glimmered in the lamplight like a rainbow across the carpet. She snatched up the closest one and straddled his hips.

Bolts of electricity tingled across her skin, while every place their skin met burst into flames. She rubbed her engorged clit over the head of that magnificent cock as she ripped open the packet and tossed the foil to the floor.

"Gabriella!" he shouted, bucking against her.

Condom in hand, she quickly sheathed him, whimpering at the shame of covering such a beautiful piece of flesh. Lodging the head against her opening, she sank down until she rested on his pelvis.

Mark braced his feet on the bed and lunged, driving deeper.

"Oh my God," she shouted and clutched at his waist to avoid being bucked off.

Now it was her turn to moan as he filled her sheath again and again in the wildest ride she'd ever been on. The tightening in her pussy grew, her lungs burned with the need for air. All of that teasing had her a hair's breadth from coming, and she wasn't going to fight the need anymore. Her vision blurred as she let go and allowed the wave to consume her. A scream rent the air, probably her own, as her mind exploded along with her heart in hard, pulsating ripples.

Between her thighs, Mark's entire body arched as he shouted, every vein and chord in his neck bulging as he joined her in orgasmic bliss. The sound of silk ties rubbing against the slats of the headboard made her sheath clamp harder around his cock, extracting every second of ecstasy until she collapsed in a boneless heap on his chest.

The fall to reality was slow and just as laborious as the ride to the heavens. Later, she'd lament the shortness of time spent on the actual intercourse. Maybe. The sonic boom at the end was well worth the quick rush to orgasm.

"Untie me." His deeply voiced command set off tremors along her spine. "I need to touch you. Feel your skin."

He wanted her to move? She almost snorted, but the idea of his arms wrapped around her was too good to pass up. Cooked noodles had more strength than her limbs right then as she struggled to sit up and reached for the ties. Her fingers fumbled as if in the beginning stages of frost bite, but still managed to untie him quickly. The knots hadn't been all that good to start with. If he had wanted to, he could have freed himself whenever he wanted. But he hadn't. He stayed true to his word as promised.

Before the last bit of silk hit the mattress, Mark's palm landed on the cheek of her ass while the other gripped her by the hair to hold her still for his kiss. Where he found this renewed strength, she hadn't a clue. It took all she had just to fight the urge to fall asleep.

He flipped her onto her back and pressed her large breasts together, sucking both nipples into his mouth at once to pull and nibble with his strong teeth while he feasted. The calluses on his hands rasped against her flesh, sending the most delicious trembles throughout her body. The scrap of his stubbled cheeks raised goose bumps as he trailed kisses down her belly.

His big hands parted her thighs and she held her breath as he looked his fill. With a lick of his lips, he dove in and sank his tongue deep into her pussy, followed by two thick fingers wedged deep into her sheath. The blunt fingertips hooked inside to press and rub, while his mouth latched onto her clit. His tongue matched the pace of his twisting fingers as the tip circled around and around.

"Mark. Oh, God. Mark. It's too much. It's too much." She tugged on his hair.

A devious chuckle was his response as he continued with the relentless motion. He didn't even pause as he looked up at her with those feral, glittering eyes, then snarled against her skin. The vibration rippled through her, and her pussy spilled more cream into his hands. The intensity in his gaze spoke volumes. He wasn't going to stop. Not until she gave him what he wanted.

She moaned as she cupped her breasts and twisted her abraded nipples. His eyes narrowed, clearly enthralled with the vision of her touching herself, but he didn't let up the sensual assault and suddenly the coil of desire snapped. Her vision dimmed and her lungs seized, burning like a bonfire behind her ribs as she screamed to the heavens.

The devilish tongue-lashing stopped, but his wicked fingers continued to massage her from the inside, priming her for more.

Mark got to his knees, the lower half of his face shining with her juices and the thick jut of his cock looking twice the size it had earlier. When her weak gaze finally met his, he pulled his fingers free then gripped his shaft, smothering it in her cream.

This was the creature he warned her about. The one who would take without mercy. Instead of frightening her, the sight of his true self stripped bare thrilled her, aroused her beyond all sense of reason. Earlier, she had said she wanted all of him. It looked like now she was about to get her wish.

Lust tightened his features as he rolled on another condom. His smothering weight as he crawled over her was more fuel on the fire. With another growl he thrust deep, spearing right to her womb. Her eyes rolled to the back of her head as she dug her manicured nails into his muscled ass. The clenching of his firm backside with each plunge and thrust drove her into delirium.

She couldn't get close enough. If it were possible to become absorbed into all that was Mark, she would have done so right then.

She pressed her lips to his ear and moaned, "You feel so good inside me, Mark. No one has ever been so deep. No one but you."

A muttered curse was her only warning before he picked up the pace. Sweat dampened his hair and dripped off the end of his nose. The bed squeaked and shuddered under the pressure of the headboard as it slammed into the wall. Her pussy fluttered, cresting for a third time.

"That's it, baby," he gritted and reared up with a roar. "Take me with you. *Take me*."

Above her, Mark bellowed like a bull, his eyes glazed over and unseeing. If not for his weight pressing her down, her entire body would have come off the mattress as she bucked and thrashed beneath him.

Never. Never. Never ever before. Had she really almost turned away from this?

Ripped from everything she had thought she'd known about passion and sex, her mind shut down, unable to assimilate the rush of emotions tearing her apart. A sob broke free, then another and another.

"God, Gabriella." Mark rolled to his side and lifted a trembling hand only to pull away. "I'm sorry, baby. I'm sorry."

Completely robbed of the ability to speak, she shook her head and grasped at his hand to drop kisses on his fingers, those oh-so-talented fingers. When the moisture finally returned to her mouth she croaked, "I'm fine. Really. I'm okay. I just. That was—it was…amazing. Totally and utterly amazing."

"Gabriella," he sighed and brushed his thumb against her lips.

The warmth in his gaze made her feel beautiful, perfect. Everything a man could want and desire. How had she ever thought his eyes were blank?

What she wouldn't give to put herself in Mark's keeping, call him her own, but she knew it was too soon to make any permanent plans for the two of them. Who was she? Just a battered woman running from her ex with nothing but the clothes on her back. The only thing she had to offer was her body, and he deserved so much more than that.

"Gabriella," he whispered before pressing his lips against hers in a kiss so tender the tears welled again. He trailed more soft kisses along her cheek and down her neck. "Gabriella," he breathed against her skin like a prayer. His palm came up to her breast for his thumb to work the tip.

She relaxed deeper into the pillow with a soft moan. One night. For one night she'd revel in the fantasy and take what she so desperately craved before dawn broke to take away everything.

Chapter Twelve

N O MATTER IF his eyes were opened or closed, all Mark saw were visions of Gabriella as she writhed naked and wild beneath him. In his ears rang the sounds of her cries, while he recalled the softness of her touch and the richness of her taste. Every moment was branded into his brain in what had been, hands down, the most fantastic night of his life.

Not even the stench of cattle and the crispness of the autumn air could cool the fire in his loins, or on his wrists. Not that he minded none.

The leather saddle creaked as he shifted in his seat. He shook his head, trying to focus on the task of driving the rest of the herd out of the hills in preparation for winter. Loading up a truck with feed and riding their dirt bikes to shepherd the herd was the quicker and more expedient method, but Trey wanted to go back to their cowboy ancestors' roots and have an old-fashioned cattle drive. Mark suspected it was a way for his friend to bond with the men he had spent years in the company of but still didn't know very much about.

All of the men were expected to pull their weight, and the last thing Mark wanted was to have to round up wayward cattle that had managed to slip away because he wasn't paying attention. Still, the image of Gabriella lying in his arms refused to go away. He loved the sight of her hair spilled across his pillow and hated that she had to leave before the sky began to change from black to dark purple. Neither of them wanted to cause gossip by having her spotted sneaking into the main house, especially when they hadn't done anything to be ashamed about, although Rafe might think differently.

That morning at the breakfast table, it had taken every ounce of control he possessed not to touch her or kiss her the moment he saw her smiling face. There had been a light in her eyes that hadn't been there the day before. An effervescence that called to him like a siren's song, and he hadn't been the only one to notice the change in her demeanor. If Jack had flirted with her for one second more, he would have found a saltshaker shoved so far up his ass, he'd be shooting grains out his nose for the rest of his life.

Even though he'd known her for just a short time, in his heart Mark knew that Gabriella was his, lock, stock, and barrel. Two people did not spontaneously combust the way they had without there being a connection at a spiritual and molecular level. What they had was beyond special, and he'd be a grade-A idiot if he didn't stake his claim and tie her to him forever.

Of course, he understood that at the moment Gabriella had a lot undecided in her life, and he liked watching her explore her independence. To a point. No matter how badly he wanted to wrap her in cotton and tell her she'd never have to worry about anything again, if he wanted to keep her, she needed to remain in control of her destiny. Hopefully, the previous evening proved she could trust him to give her what she needed.

With the reminder of the night before, the ache in his groin and wrists flared, making him grimace.

"Hey, Hoss, are you okay?" Trey asked, urging his horse into a trot to catch up with him.

"I'm fine."

"You looked like you were in pain or something."

Mark kept his mouth shut and his eyes on the herd. From the corner of his eye he saw Trey continue to stare. Those blue eyes narrowed as if to bore a hole into his head in an attempt to pick his brain. Well, let him keep picking.

"You have to tell me," Trey demanded a quarter of a mile down the trail later.

From under the brim of his hat, he slid Trey a long sideways glance. "Tell you what?"

"You know."

"Don't have a clue, Hoss." He chomped down on the wad of gum in his mouth.

Trey tipped his hat back. "I saw Gabriella sneak into the house early this morning, looking like she was rode hard and put away wet. Maybe I should ask Jack."

"Shut the fuck up," Mark snapped, then looked around to confirm that Jack was still upfront riding point while Ben and Adam had the rear. Thankfully, Rafe was with Colby clear across the way, taking the left side.

He turned on Trey with a glare that should have dropped the man dead. "Don't talk about her that way."

"Look, normally I couldn't care less about your women. Well, not care less, but you know what I mean. Gabriella is my guest, and she's recently suffered a trauma. I need to make sure you aren't going to hurt her." He held up a hand when Mark growled. "I know, you wouldn't do it intentionally, but have you really given any thought about what getting involved with her means?"

"Of course I have. I know she's got things she needs to work out, choices to make, but I won't pressure her. If she decides she wants me to be a part of her future, that'd be more than all right with me. For now, I'm gonna be there for her, however she wants me."

Trey nodded then looked across the herd. "Now I have to figure out how to keep you alive when Rafe finds out."

That made him chuckle. "I'll take care of Rafe."

"Okay. Sure. That's a relief."

Mark grinned at his sarcasm. "She's an adult, and Rafe will have to get used to her making her own decisions."

"You are so asking to be killed."

Mark continued to face forward as Trey shook his head, probably already planning his funeral. Didn't bother him none. The only opinion Mark cared about was Gabriella's.

The back of his neck tickled as Trey continued to stare in his direction. He'd known Trey long enough to know his curiosity wasn't satisfied. By the same token, Trey should be well aware that Mark wasn't gonna talk unless under duress. The only sound for the longest time was the clopping of hooves and the snapping of his gum.

"Was it good?" Trey asked.

Best he ever had, but he was never gonna tell Trey that. Sure, part of him wanted to brag about the hours of pleasure he gave her, but his woman deserved better than to be locker-room gossip. Even though it was really, really, really good gossip.

The ache between his legs made him shift in his seat, which pulled the cuffs of his coat across his wrists. He closed his eyes as he breathed through the sting of discomfort.

"What's wrong with you?" Trey asked. "You keep making that face."

"It's nothing." He shifted his shoulders, trying to relieve the pressure on the oversensitive skin.

"It looks like you got the clap or something."

"Got experience with that, Hoss?" Mark joked and continued to look into the distance, hoping his ears weren't as red-hot as they felt.

Apparently they were, as Trey nudged his horse closer. Even the dog running beside them yipped with interest. "What did you do?"

"Nothing."

"Don't bullshit me. What did you do? What did you do? What did you do? What did you do?" He kept the chant going for a full minute. He was loud enough, and insistent enough, that the other hands turned to look in their direction with open curiosity.

"Shut up," Mark snarled. Damn it. Why did Trey have to be so nosy?

Maybe because Trey's always been a nosy bastard.

At least he was before his son died. After that he had lost interest in, well, everything. Mark guessed this was even more proof the old Trey was back. Which meant he was not going to drop the subject.

He glanced around again and lowered his already deep voice to a murmur. "I let Gabriella live out a fantasy she's had."

Interest sparked in Trey's eyes. "What kind of fantasy?"

"I, uh, let her tie me to the bed. Ended up with a bit of a fabric burn on my wrists. That's all," he gritted out.

Trey's eyes narrowed for a second before they bulged out of his sockets. His mouth fell open and worked up and down as he tried to form sound. When he caught his breath, he let loose with a laugh so loud, it echoed off the hills and bent him double over the saddle horn.

"Glad to be of some amusement," Mark muttered and urged his horse into a short gallop to escape the hysterical laughter.

"Hold up, hold up," Trey called out and raced to catch up. "I'm sorry I laughed. I can't believe you let her do that. Wow.

That's—that's pretty ballsy, man." He pointed a gloved finger at Mark's frown. "Don't give me that look. You know that if it were me, you'd be laughing too and telling everyone else about it in excruciating detail."

Fuck. He had him there.

"Does it really hurt that bad?"

"No. Not really."

"Let me see."

"No."

"Come on. Let me see. Let me see. Let me see. Let me see."

"Oh, for fuck's sake." Mark pulled the cuff back over his left wrist. Two-inch wide red bands circled both his wrists like he'd been sitting on the sun's surface. Luckily, most of the swelling had gone down and all of the mobility had come back that morning.

Trey let loose with a low whistle. "Does the other one look like that too?" When Mark nodded, Trey tipped his head back and howled like a banshee.

Mark left him in a cloud of dust, riding up ahead where the only creatures around to disturb him were the hundred-plus head of cattle.

Trey gave him all of five minutes before he caught up. "You cannot share things like that with me and not expect me to react."

The pop of his gum was Mark's only response.

"Was it worth it?" Trey asked quietly.

"Yeah. She was worth it."

This time his laughter was more of relief than of teasing. "Good. That's good. I'm happy for you, Hoss. She didn't have any traumatic flashbacks?" Mark shook his head and Trey's smile broadened. "Even better. You know, I think you'd be good for her. And I think she could be good for you too. Greta already loves her to pieces. I really hope it works out for you guys."

"Thanks, Hoss."

Although it wasn't required, having his friend's approval lifted a weight off his shoulders. During the period of time Mark had harbored feelings for Greta, a wall had come up between him and his best friend that had been a burden for so long, he had gotten used to holding his thoughts under his hat. He had had to maintain his feelings so as not to intrude on any reconciliation for the two people he loved most in the world, despite the many times he wanted to wake them both up to what was going on around them. Trey might not have noticed just how big the rift between the two of them had become during the drama, but Mark had. He had missed his friend, more than he realized. It was good to finally have something to talk about with him besides cattle.

"So what's your plan to woo the fair lady?" Trey asked. "I mean for something deeper than a one-night stand."

"Just give her what she needs, when she asks. And especially when she doesn't. Take it one day at a time." He winked. "Right, Hoss?"

Trey laughed at the reminder of his mantra. "Good words to live by. And don't worry, there is no way I'm telling Rafe you're doing his sister."

"You're what!"

Oh…shit.

Mark closed his eyes and bit back another curse. With a weary sigh, he turned to face a seething volcano of outrage perched on top of a fourteen-hands high mare. The disbelief and horror in Rafe's expression indicated just how much he'd overheard.

"Hey, guys." Trey turned his horse toward the quartet of riders behind them. His smile was on the overly bright side as he asked, "What's up?"

Rafe's furious gaze never left Mark's face. "You fucked my sister?"

Mark flinched at both the outrage in his tone and his choice of words. Was this the best way to break the news to Rafe? Of course not, and he understood why the man might be upset. But he was not going to allow what he had with Gabriella sound dirty and shameful in any way.

"Rafe, you should know that I think your sister is an amazing woman. But what happens between us has nothing to do with you."

"Noooo," Ben groaned the second before Rafe launched off his horse, soaring over the four feet of distance separating them and tackling Mark to the ground.

The combination of the hard earth and the weight of a pissed-off brother knocked the gum right out of Mark's mouth and made stars dance in his vision. As he struggled to make sense of up and down, Rafe scrambled to his knees and grabbed him by the front of the shirt. Rafe's first punch caught him in the mouth, busting his lip open in a little explosion of blood. The second one landed on his jaw and could have broken bone if Ben hadn't pulled Rafe off before his fist fully connected.

The clang of distressed cattle and imaginary bells rang in his ears as Adam and Colby scooped him under the arms and pulled him to his feet. For several seconds, he rocked on his heels until the world stopped spinning. It had been a while since he had taken a hit to the head. Yep. Still hurt.

"Keep your hands off my sister, you filthy son of a bitch!" Rafe struggled in Ben's hold, spitting and hurling curses in English and Spanish.

Trey stepped in front of the irate Latino with his palms out in a gesture of peace. "Rafe. You've gotta calm down and use your head."

"He touched my sister!"

"She hog-tied him to the bed," Trey shouted.

Neither man nor beast made a sound as the world came to a screeching halt. Every drop of blood drained from Mark's face to churn in his gut. He hoped Trey's health insurance was up to date, because Mark was about to break every bone in his body. As soon as his double vision cleared.

Rafe was the first to blink. "What?"

"What are you doing, Hoss?" Mark gritted out between clenched teeth.

Trey waved him away. "Now listen, Rafe. Your sister is old enough to make her own choices. You might not like it, but it's a fact you're gonna have to face sooner or later. And you know what kind of man Mark is. She couldn't be in safer hands. Look at him." He stomped over and grabbed Mark by the jacket and yanked his sleeve up to expose the angry welts around his wrists. "He cared so much about making her happy that he let her tie him to his own bed. Now he's in agonizing pain. Would he do that if he didn't care about her?"

Mark furrowed his brow at the "agonizing pain" comment. Trey pinched his lips together, and he motioned with his eyes to play along. Although it galled the hell out of him to appear weak, Mark grimaced and gingerly tugged his sleeve back into place. Truthfully, his face hurt worse than his wrists, and even that was now bearable.

"Now, if we're done here, let's round up the strays and keep going," Trey continued. "The ladies are preparing something special for us tonight, and I don't want to keep them waiting."

Rafe looked Mark over with a scrutinizing gaze. "Your wrists hurt?"

He nodded. "Like they're on fire."

"Good." He stepped into Mark's grill and jammed a finger into his chest. "You hurt my sister, and I'll kill you."

"I understand why you're worried, Rafe, I do. I promise, I won't hurt her."

"No offense, but the last asshole who promised me that beat the shit out of her," he snarled and stomped away.

With a heavy heart, Mark watched as Gabriella's brother climbed onto his horse with an angry snap to his movements and took off at a full gallop. This was not how he wanted his relationship with Gabriella to be revealed.

He probed the split portion of his lip and winced. If that was how Rafe reacted, what in the hell was Gabriella gonna do when she found out everyone at the ranch now knew about their night together?

Chapter Thirteen

"YOU'RE FUCKING MY boss?"

Gabriella froze with the knife in her hand hovering over a creamy blob of beignet dough. She glanced up to see Rafe standing in the kitchen doorway, his black hair sticking out in different directions and a flush streaking his cheeks. The tight line of his mouth stood out against his tanned skin in a white slash. If she had to guess, the cat was out of the bag and climbing the curtains with freshly sharpened claws.

For a brief moment, her fingers tightened around the handle of the knife, but she resisted the urge to fling the blade at her overbearing brother. She turned to Greta, who was watching them with wide-eyed interest. "Will you please excuse me while I have a moment alone with my brother?"

"Are you going to take that knife with you?" Greta asked with a teasing grin.

Maybe.

She calmly set the knife on the cutting board and motioned for Rafe to follow her down the hall to Trey's empty office and shut the door behind them.

Before she could draw a breath, Rafe laid into her. "What are you thinking, Lita? Did you really think banging my boss is a good idea? And don't bother to deny it," he said when she opened her mouth to do just that. "I heard him and Trey talking about you."

Flames hit her cheeks as she sucked in her breath. Mark was talking to Trey about her? About them? And Rafe overheard? Oh God, who else overheard?

She slumped against the office door and stifled a groan. It wasn't that she was ashamed of what they had done, but their time alone together was private, not fodder for the cattle drive. Hadn't there been anything else to talk about? Football? Weather? The fit of their cowboy hats?

While the possible topics of Mark and Trey's conversation ran through her mind, Rafe continued his rant. Too late, she realized Trey's office might not have been the best location for their discussion with the potential projectiles of picture frames, books, and knickknacks within reaching distance.

"How can you even think of getting involved with anyone else?" Rafe yelled. "You're a battered woman, for Pete's sake!"

Oh, no he didn't.

"I am *not* a battered woman," she said, breaking into his tirade with a calm, unyielding voice. "I was hurt, but that does not define who I am. What do you want me to do, Rafe? Forget that I'm a woman? Forget that I'm a human being with needs, and wants, and desires?" His lips twisted at the mention of her desires, but she continued. "I didn't ask for what happened to me, and I didn't ask to have Mark come into my life when he did. Could the timing have been better? Maybe. Probably. But I can't change the past. The way you talk makes it sound like I should stay locked away forever. That I should live in fear forever. When I'm with Mark, I feel safe. I feel whole. He doesn't treat me like I'm broken. Because I'm not. I'm not broken, Rafe. Stop treating me like I am."

Right before her eyes, he deflated as if she had cut the end off a blown-up balloon. All of his outrage evaporated, leaving a tired, haggard man in his place.

"Lita. *Mija.*" He rubbed his hand over his face. "I'm sorry. I don't think you're broken. I just don't want to see you hurt again. I can't."

"I understand. Which is why you're still standing and not on the floor." She crossed to him and wrapped her arms around his lean waist, resting her head on his chest. When he returned her hug, she smiled against his jacket. "Just be there for me, Rafe. That's all I need."

"I will. And Mark knows that, too. I won't hesitate to beat him down again if he hurts you."

Her head snapped up. "Again?"

The red rose again in his cheeks, and his gaze skittered away while his Adam's apple bobbed hard with a swallow.

"What did you do?" When he didn't answer right away, she bunched the front of his shirt in her fist. "Rafael Javier Domingo Montoya, what did you do?"

"I, uh, well." He huffed out a breath. "What do you think I did, Lita? I punched him."

"What?"

"Twice."

"*Oh, Dios mio.*" She pushed him away. "You punched your boss? Is he okay? Where is he?"

"Probably his house," he muttered.

Shooting him a glare, she rushed out of the office and flew through the kitchen to grab her boots from the mudroom. "Hey, Greta?" she called out. "Just cover that dough for me, or better yet, make Rafe fry them. I'll be back in a minute." She didn't wait for a response before dashing out the door.

Once on Mark's porch, she knocked on the door. When an answer didn't come right away, her concern turned to genuine fear. Rafe had a tendency to channel the Incredible Hulk when he was angry, and he was capable of causing a lot of damage before he realized what he'd done. That trait was why he worked better with livestock than people.

"Mark?" She forwent the polite knock and pounded on the door. "Mark!"

The sound of footsteps slightly alleviated her worry, mainly because that didn't necessarily mean they were his. The door opened and she sent a prayer to the heavens that he was standing on his own two feet. A shaft of weak sunlight highlighted the side of his face.

She covered her mouth with a gasp. "Oh, Mark, I am so sorry. I didn't mean for this to happen."

The uninjured corner of his mouth quirked up. "Li'l Bit, this was not your fault. Come on in. It's too cold to be running around without a coat." He tugged her into the living room before he shut the door. "I'm the one who should apologize. I shouldn't have let Trey get so nosy. He saw you entering the house this morning and was asking me about it and Rafe overheard. I'm sorry if you were embarrassed in any way."

Well... This was unexpected. Sad but true. Mark was a man from another time, and only on rare occasions had she seen a man behave with such honor. Should she smile when he acted in such a fashion, or cry because there were too few men like him on the planet? At least in her world there were too few.

Had been too few. Not were. Had been. New start, better friends.

"I'll be all right." Not indifferent to his injuries, she gave him a light hug. "Have you put ice on that yet?" She turned to walk into the kitchen.

"Gabriella." He caught her hand. His gaze skipped away and a flush crept over his cheeks in a way that made her heart lurch.

He licked his lips and said, "During the fight, it kinda came out about what I let you do to me last night. The tying up and stuff."

"What? You mean they know—they *all* know that I—" she slapped a hand over her mouth. No wonder Rafe was spitting nails. He had just found out his baby sister was kinky.

"I'm sorry." Mark held her around the biceps. "I wasn't gonna tell anyone. Then Trey noticed I was sore and we started talking, then Rafe overheard us and blew a gasket. That's when Trey ups and blurts out that I let you hog-tie me. He figured it would show Rafe what I was willing to do to make you happy. But now all I've done is make your brother angry and humiliate you—why are you laughing?"

She sucked in her lips and choked down another giggle. He looked so miserable, she didn't think he'd find it funny that she found his apology humorous because it was the most she'd ever heard him say in a single shot. The poor man was most definitely sorry.

"Mark, I understand it was all a, well, let's just call it an unfortunate set of circumstances." She took him by the hand and led him to the kitchen table. Pushing down on his shoulders, she made him sit then searched for a dishtowel. She wet one with water, then filled the pocket of fabric with ice from the freezer.

"You're not mad at me?" he asked with a confused crinkle of his brow.

"No. I know you didn't do anything on purpose." She placed the ice against his jaw with a gentle touch. "Besides, I think you paid plenty enough for my embarrassment."

"It wasn't nearly enough."

The adamancy in his tone told her he truly meant what he said. She placed a gentle kiss on the worst of the bruising before she replaced the ice. The iciness of his skin numbed her lips. "I forgive you."

He reached out and grasped her by the hips, drawing her down to settle astride his lap. His big, circular belt buckle pressed right against her core, sending a shot of the warm fuzzies up her spine. "You're a good woman, with a hell of a protector for a brother."

"Thank you, Mr. Webber." She carefully placed a kiss to the corner of his mouth.

As she moved to pull away, he reached up and cradled her head at the nape of her neck. He pressed for a deeper kiss then pulled back with a wince. "The little bugger is keeping me from kissing you properly. I'll have to get him back for that."

"Mark."

"I'm teasing." He winked. "Mostly."

He took the ice from her hand and set it on the table before pressing a kiss to the tips of her fingers. He settled her hand against his chest then nestled her head against his shoulder, engulfing her in his strong arms. "Tell me about your day. What kind of trouble were you and Greta getting into?"

She relaxed in his warm, masculine embrace, sinking in to the sensuous massage of his fingers on her scalp. "I didn't do a whole lot. Greta and I have been preparing for the cookout for most of the day. And I checked online for any job opportunities."

Under her cheek his chest froze as his breath caught. "Where were you looking?"

"All over. Ellensburg, Yakima, Spokane, even Portland."

"Did you try looking here in Mission?"

She sensed more than heard the tension behind the query. "There's not a whole lot around here. But Greta did say I can use their address to establish a residence on my applications, so it would make sense to look for something close by."

He tilted her chin up with his fingers. "I'd like it if you

stayed here."

His deep gaze made her heart pound as a roar filled her ears. When he looked at her that way, all she could see were his dark eyes, firm lips, and a promise of forever.

"Mark, what are we doing?" she whispered.

"I'm holding you."

"No." She pushed away then stood, crossing her arms in front of her chest. "What are we doing? What is this? Am I a diversion or a fling? I'm not ready for any type of relationship, if you're suggesting one, which you haven't, but sometimes I think you are. Maybe. Possibly. Crap. I'm confusing myself."

He got to his feet and moved toward her in slow, controlled steps. He settled his hands on her shoulders but made no motion to pull her closer. "I like you, Gabriella. I like spending time with you. Do I know where this will go? No. But I do know I want more than just one night. All I can say is we'll just take it one day at a time."

"One day at a time?"

"Yep."

"That's it? Is it really that simple?"

"Does it have to be difficult?" He half-smiled around his swollen lip.

She laughed at that. "I guess not."

He cradled her cheek, and his palm was so warm, she wanted to nuzzle it like she was a kitten. He pushed a lock of hair off her face, and he placed another tender kiss to her lips. "Ah, darlin'. As much as I'd love to stay in and have you kiss my bruises, we should probably make an appearance at dinner before Rafe knocks down my door."

"Good idea."

Like a true gentleman, he escorted her to the front door and gestured for her to precede him. When he caught up to her on the top step, he paused and looked down at her for several long seconds before he held out his hand.

In the lavender twilight, with the last of the sun's rays lighting his palm, the significance of the action made her heart kick in her chest. If she took his hand, and they walked into the house together, she knew they'd be making a statement that'd be as real as if he branded her.

Did she want Mark to stake his claim?

Please don't let me regret this.

With a small prayer, she slid her hand into his.

Chapter Fourteen

"MAGPIE, I DON'T think it gets any better than this." Trey wrapped Greta in his arms and lowered his head to nuzzle behind her ear.

"Just think, the night's still young." She kissed his whiskered chin.

Gabriella watched the loving couple as they basked in the campfire's glow and wondered if she'd ever find someone who loved her like Trey obviously did Greta.

Mark sat beside her on a fallen log and motioned for her to sit next to him, allowing him to pull her into the cradle of his body. Rafe scowled at them from across the flames, but kept his mouth shut. She gifted him with a grateful smile and relaxed into Mark's embrace.

The starry night sky was the perfect backdrop to celebrate the end of the cattle drive. One would have thought they were celebrating with the population of the entire town, considering the spread Trey and Greta had laid out. Gabriella had never seen so much food consumed by so few people. After attending countless parties where no one ate and every conversation held a double meaning, this gathering of friends, who actually cared about each other, was a much-welcomed change.

To their right, Ben plucked a melody on his guitar that added a mystical vibe to the misty evening. Jack and Adam were behind them arguing about the BCS standings, and Colby watched them all from the picnic table with a dish of apple cobbler in his hand and a contented smile on his face.

"Hey, Hoss. Can you hand me a beer?" Mark asked Trey.

"Sure." He pulled a long neck from the cooler beside him and tossed it to Mark. "There you go, Hoss."

"Why do you call each other 'Hoss'?" Gabriella asked, then promptly forgot the question as she became enthralled with the way the muscles of Mark's throat worked as he swallowed his beer.

He licked at a drop of brew that clung to his lip. "Do you remember that old show *Bonanza*?"

Huh. What? Oh, right. "Sure. My mom watched it."

He nodded. "Ever since we were kids, Trey and I have been battling it out over who gets to be Little Joe."

"So if you call him Hoss," she said, following his train of thought. "Then by default you're claiming to be Little Joe, and vice versa?"

"Yep."

"And you're been doing that for years?"

"Yep."

She shook her head. "I really do not understand men."

His chuckle buzzed along her skin as his lips brushed her cheek. "Yeah, it drives Greta crazy too. Do you have any other nicknames besides 'Lita'?"

She nuzzled his jaw with her nose. Nestled in his arms with the softness of her sheep skin coat surrounding her, she never felt so at peace. "Nope, none."

"What about 'Gabby'?"

"Ugh." She made a gagging sound. "Do not call me that. When I worked at the country club, people called me Gabby. It was only because they were too lazy to say 'Gabriella.' "

"I like how you say your name. You make it sound exotic. Do you know a lot of Spanish?"

"Not a whole lot. My parents tried to teach us. We know enough to get by."

"I find it really sexy." His heavy lidded gaze warmed her up some more.

"Hmm, I guess I'll have to work on it, *corazón.*"

He lowered his head and his lips brushed hers when Rafe spoke in a loud voice from above them. "Can I get you guys anything to drink? Preferably something ice cold?"

"We're fine. Thank you, Rafe," she said as she gave him the evil eye from beneath her lashes. When the big lug continued to stare as if he could physically part them by glare alone she added, "You may go now. Really. Go. Now."

He grunted, and his lip curled in a snarl, but he turned to take his seat across the way.

"He worries because he loves you," Mark murmured in her ear.

"I know. Which is why I'm only mildly annoyed with him."

"Gabriella?" he whispered.

"Hmm?" She snuggled against him with a sigh, trying to recapture the mood Rafe disrupted.

"Will you go with me to the Harvest Festival?"

Her eyes flew open. "What?"

"The Harvest Festival. Every year there's a party at Martinez's Orchard. Kind of an end of harvest–Halloween thing the entire town looks forward to every year. Would you go with me?"

"Like a date?"

"Yeah."

Right. Dating. Dinners out and movies. A ritual that usually happens before sex, which was probably why she didn't recognize the question for what it was.

Only the Harvest Festival didn't sound like it'd be just a normal date. Was she ready to meet the people of Mission as Mark's girlfriend?

"Gabriella?"

The vulnerability in his eyes and hint of insecurity that pinched his lips made her realize just how much her answer meant to him. "Yes."

Uncertainty turned to joy as he smiled. "Yeah?"

"Yeah," she sighed. If she was going to "be with Mark," then she was going to be with Mark, 100 percent. She needed to get her head out of her ass and just take the risk.

Besides, she loved the way he smiled at her, as if he couldn't wait to get her alone and fulfill the promise in his sexy gaze. And all because she said yes.

"Are you gonna get that?" he asked.

She blinked with confusion. "Get what?"

"Your coat is buzzing."

"What?" Was that a code for something?

He patted her pocket and laughed. "Your coat is buzzing."

"Oh. I forgot I had my phone with me." What a goober. And here she thought that pleasant vibration was caused by being in his company. She searched through the pockets and pulled out her cell. Lost in Mark's smile, she didn't look at the display as she answered, "Hello?"

"You've been a bad girl, Gabby."

Chapter Fifteen

W ITH A CRY, Gabriella hurled the phone across the yard. The black rectangle hit the side of the barn and clattered to the ground.

"Gabriella?" Mark's hands tightened on her hips. "What is it?"

Even across the yard, she could hear as the phone again began to vibrate with an incoming call and the display glowed with an eerie yellow light in the dark. She leapt from her seat and ran to kneel beside the offending object, reaching for the nearest rock and smashing the phone over and over until all that was left were bits of plastic.

"Idiot. I'm such an idiot," she muttered as tears burned hot trails down her cheeks. She fell back against the side of the barn and dropped her head into her hands. Mark was by her side a second later, with Rafe and the others hot on his heels.

"Gabriella? Sweetheart?" He pulled her hands down. "Gabriella?" He cupped her face in his palms, encouraging her to meet his gaze. "Let me guess. Drew."

"How was that bastard able to call you?" Rafe's scowl matched Mark's. "I thought the police gave you that phone."

They had. A lovely prepaid phone with a number known only to those involved with her case. And apparently now Drew.

"I'm such an idiot," she muttered, lost in her waking nightmare. "I thought I could just leave and that would be it. He'd leave me alone, and I'd get my fucking life back. I am so stupid." She scrambled to her feet and found all avenues of escape blocked by six cowboys and a woman who stared at her with identical expressions of pity and concern. "I have to go. He'll come for me. I have to go now." The panic in her voice rose with each escalating beat of her heart.

"Hush, baby, shh." Mark pulled her stiff body into an embrace and smoothed his hands up and down her back, but not even his gentle touch stopped her from shuddering. "It's okay. Just calm down. He doesn't know where you are. And even if he did, he can't harm you here."

"Yes, he can. He'll find me and hurt me." She pushed at his chest, kicking her way free from his hold, and felt the pull of hysteria dragging her beneath the surface of sanity, stealing her breath. "He'll hurt everyone. Greta," she gasped, and pointed toward the other woman. "He could hurt Greta and the baby. I can't—I can't let that happen. I have to go."

Mark blocked her way, his hands raised. "Hold up, Gabriella. Just stop. Breathe. Breathe, damn it, and stop."

"I can't." Her throat closed up and a rubber band seemed to tighten around her lungs as she sputtered and fell to her knees.

What was wrong with her? Why couldn't she breathe? Why did everywhere she look, all she saw were the buttercream-colored walls of her old bedroom and not the endless expanse of night sky? Why was the scent of her ex-husband's expensive cologne filling her nose and not the aroma of campfire and livestock? And why couldn't she stop these fucking tears from streaming from her eyes as if she'd turned on a faucet?

"Rafe?" A note of desperation tinged Mark's request.

"Lita, honey, I'm right here." Her brother reached out his

hand, settling his palm on her back as she curled into a ball. "You're safe. I'm here. We're here. Nothing's gonna get ya."

Mark joined them, kneeling beside her in the mud. Both men cradled her as she rocked back and forth, fighting her way free from the terror that had its clutches sunk deep within her mind.

She had no idea how long they sat on the cold, soggy ground. Minutes, hours, lifetimes. It might have been seconds, but it was long enough for her joints to ache from being bent in an awkward position and for her head to pound as if she had beaten it against the wall. Throughout it all, Rafe and Mark cooed and murmured words of encouragement while keeping her warm with their heat.

When her sobs began to quiet, Mark tilted up her chin to meet his gentle gaze. "You have nothing to fear while you're here, darlin'. If he sets foot on the ranch, we'll know. He wants you scared. He wants you out on your own. But you're not gonna give him what he wants, are ya? Because you're strong. You're the girl that told that bastard no." He brushed the hair from her forehead and wiped at her cheeks with a handkerchief he pulled from his back pocket. "You don't have to be afraid because you're not alone. You're not alone this time. You understand me? You are not alone."

More tears fell, but no longer were they from fear. A knight in the most sparkling, shiny armor ever welded had nothing on Mark and the fierce determination in his gaze. He had faith in her, believed in her power, and more important, was ready to stand by her.

She blinked to clear her vision and met Rafe's concerned gaze. "I love you," he mouthed.

"I love you too," she mouthed back.

"Mark's right, Gabriella," Trey said, holding Greta in his arms. By the light of the bonfire, Gabriella saw the tracks of the woman's tears on her cheeks. "There's no better place for you to be than here. We'll watch out for you."

"I appreciate what you're saying." She pulled away from Mark and stood, wincing when her knees popped. All she could think was that Drew was going to come after her. While part of her knew there was no place safer to be than the ranch, the other part wanted to run far away and leave all of these nice people in peace. "But I really don't want to bring trouble to the ranch."

"If you leave, I'll bring you back myself," Greta said. "You're staying, and that's that."

"See?" Mark nudged her arm. "You're staying."

"Thank you." She tried to smile, but even her cheeks were too sore to do much more than flinch. "I'm sorry to have freaked out like that."

"We don't blame you one bit." Greta came over to give her a brief hug. "I'd have probably reacted the same way, except I would have thrown the phone in the fire. Do you need anything? A tissue? Stiff drink?"

"No, but thank you." She gave Greta another squeeze in gratitude.

"Hey, guys," Ben's deep bass boomed across the yard. "Let's give the girl room to breathe. Why don't we clean up here and see what game is on."

The men dispersed and began to pick up trash while Trey worked on breaking up the bonfire.

Another wave of embarrassment washed over her. "I'm sorry I wrecked your party."

"You did no such thing," Greta said. "It was time to take in this food anyway. Or I should say these empty plates. We did good, girl."

Gabriella took a step forward to do her share in the cleanup but was stopped by Mark's hand on her arm. He pinched her chin between his thumb and finger. "It's okay to be scared, Gabriella. But know that I won't let anything happen to you."

She loved how he was ready to fight her demons, but she had to start standing on her own two feet. "This isn't your battle, Mark."

Fire flashed in his eyes. "I'm making it mine."

"Mark—"

"Haven't you figured it out yet? That you mean more to me than a night of hot sex?"

Somehow she managed a genuine smile. "I'm figuring that out."

"That's 'cause you're a smart girl." His thumb brushed her lower lip. "Stay with me tonight. Please."

The impulse was to say no. It wasn't appropriate. They still barely knew each other. But there was nothing she wanted more at that moment than to spend the night in his arms. "I'd love to."

The corner of his mouth curled up, and then slowly spread into a smile that set firecrackers off in her tummy while soothing her frazzled nerves at the same time.

"I'd be kissing your socks off right now, but I think your brother wants to make sure you're okay. I'll be close." He dropped a kiss on her nose and turned her to face the somber-looking man behind her.

"Come here, kid." Rafe pulled her into a fierce hug.

"I'm okay, really. I was just caught off guard."

"I know. You're too tough to let one phone call upset you for very long. Do you want to stay with me tonight?"

Oh, this could go poorly. "Actually, I'm staying with Mark."

He pulled back with a disapproving grunt. "Is this about you being a woman with," his lip curled, "desires?"

"Sort of. I just...really like being with him."

"I don't like it, but that's only because you're my sister." He heaved a put-upon sigh. "Mark's a good guy. I know he'll look out for you."

"I appreciate your understanding." She stood on tiptoe to kiss his cheek. "Come on, let's do our share and help out."

They gathered the last of the dishes and took them into the house. In no time, everything was put away and the ranch hands had settled in front of the big-screen TV watching the Washington football game. The sight of all those men crammed on couches and sprawled on the floor was another reminder of the special relationship the men of the Sprawling A had with each other.

When Gabriella was growing up on her family's farm, the few hands they employed would work their shift, then take off to town or move on to the next job at the end of the day. It was the same on the neighboring farms as well. This tight sense of family on the Armstrong ranch was as beautiful as it was rare.

But as close as the men were, there was one in particular who appeared ready to be separated from the herd.

"Ready to head to my place?" Mark asked.

"Let me just get a few things," she said before rushing up to her room.

She made quick work of brushing her teeth and removing her makeup. The bruises on her face had faded enough that they were easily covered with a tinted moisturizer. She rolled a silk nightgown in midnight blue and a pair of panties for the next morning into a cylinder shape that fit into her coat pocket then ran downstairs.

"In here," came Mark's voice from the kitchen where he waited, all alone. He nodded at her empty hands. "I thought you were collecting a few things?"

"I did. I have everything I need right here." She patted her coat pocket.

His confused expression melted into one of desire. "Ready then?" He held out his hand.

Who'd have thought that the big, tough cowboy was so into holding hands?

She placed her hand in his. His fingers closed around her palm as he bent to place a kiss on the back. "Let's go."

ALL OF HER earlier tension melted away the moment she walked into Mark's home. The floor lamp was on in the corner as always, spreading a welcoming golden glow across the entryway. The light combined with the comforting scent of Mark's aftershave mixed with the firewood stacked near the hearth and eased the tension in her muscles. Keeping his hand in hers, he led her up the stairs to his bedroom.

"Just make yourself at home," he offered before disappearing into the bathroom.

A second later, she heard the rush of water running from the faucet along with all of the other noises that came from a man preparing for bed. It was nice. Homey. Just so darn normal that her cells soaked it up and kicked the last of her stress to the curb. She changed into her nightie and folded her clothes, placing them in a neat pile on top of the dresser before slipping under the fluffy comforter. Near her head lay a twisted piece of blue fabric tied to the bed frame. Man, they really had done a number on those neckties. No wonder Mark's wrists were so chafed.

He came back into the room and stripped off his undershirt, then tossed it into the hamper in the corner. When he turned around and saw her in bed, he froze. The muscles in his face relaxed, while his eyes focused on her with an intensity that made her throat close up.

She straightened in alarm and squeaked out, "What's wrong?"

"You—ah…you look really good in my bed." The deep rumble in his voice made her shiver under the down comforter.

Without breaking his gaze, he lifted his hands to the buttons on his jeans. The flex of his muscles as he slowly slid the jeans down his legs fascinated her to no end. She couldn't help but smile at the appearance of his black briefs, but the grin was short lived as she promptly choked when she saw the thick stalk of his arousal.

"I do love the way you look at me," he mumbled and slid under the covers next to her. "And I love this nightgown." He ran his broad hand over her shoulder and down between her breasts, pausing over the flat of her tummy. She leaned forward and nuzzled her cheek against his bare chest. "Gabriella, you know I didn't ask you over here only to make love with you."

"You mean I have more to look forward to?"

His laugh rumbled under her ear. "I wanted to give you a place to rest without having to worry about anything."

Oooh. What a charmer. He'd better be careful. If he kept saying things like that, she'd be in love with him by dawn.

Would that be such a terrible thing?

Maybe. Depended on which way the cookie crumbled.

She pushed away the thought and placed a kiss over his heart. "Thank you."

The silky fabric of her gown caught on his calloused palms as he smoothed his hands over her body. "This feels so nice under my palms. Jesus, Gabriella. You are so sexy."

Any witty comeback she might have said was swallowed by his kiss and the purr that rattled from the back of her throat. He didn't rush his kiss, didn't hurry, or delve deeper. It was as if he had all the time in the world to taste her. Those magic hands of his kneaded and plumped her breasts, while he rained hot kisses along her chin and down to the soft swell of flesh above the lace of her gown. While he licked and tickled her flesh with the tip of his tongue, she relaxed deeper into the pillows and sifted his hair through her fingers, watching the play of light in the blue-black strands. Her limbs grew heavy and languid under his lazy exploration even as his stubbled chin burned her skin as he buried his face in her cleavage.

"I love your tit—breasts," he corrected, then suckled a nipple through the dark silk.

Her back arched on an inhale and she pressed deeper into his hold. She loved the satin texture of his skin over his heated muscles as she squeezed and massaged his arms and back. She skimmed her fingertips down his washboard abs to his cotton-covered erection.

"I think you'll be more comfortable without these." She raked her fingernails over his straining shaft.

"You don't mind?" He smiled and those adorable dimples made an appearance.

"Not at all."

He jumped out of bed, stripped, and was back under the covers before the mattress stopped bouncing.

She giggled. "Eager much?" This playful side of him was so much fun.

"Yep." He lay back with his hands behind his head. "As you were, ma'am. As you were."

Oh yeah. She was definitely falling for him. Hard.

Well, if he was ready to play, she was more than ready to bring her "A" game. The objective? Drive him out of his mind.

She gripped him firmly around the base of his cock and stroked up and down as she licked a path down the strong column of his neck to the cinnamon-colored points of his nipples. By the way he jumped, she guessed having his nipples sucked was a new experience for him.

"Ah, that feels so fu—good," he bit out.

There it was again.

She popped off his chest. "Why are you doing that?"

"Doing what?" he moaned with a shift of his hips, silently begging her to continue stroking the hot staff throbbing in her hand.

"You keep censoring yourself? Why?"

He opened his eyes and looked at her as if the answer were obvious. "You don't deserve having me spout vulgarities at you. You're classier than that."

Was he for real? "But you were swearing all over the place last night."

A flash of what looked like shame darkened his features as he broke her gaze. "Last night was amazing, but I shouldn't have lost control like that. I should have been more gentle. I'm sorry."

The idea that he thought she should be offended by the way he expressed his passion almost made her laugh until she realized he was serious.

Really? Here she was, brushing her thumb over the head of his cock and her saliva dying on his nipples, and he thought she would be upset because he told her he liked her tits? Wasn't this the same man who told her to embrace her strength and that she had the courage to conquer anything? Apparently he needed to learn that she could be strong in the bedroom too.

"Mark. I like sex. And I like fucking." His cock jerked in her hand. Hmmm. So he liked to hear her talk dirty, did he? "I want you to tell me how much you enjoy my touch, my body. And I want you to tell me in whatever words, or sounds, or actions you choose. I want all of you, Mark."

In his eyes she saw a glimmer of doubt that she was telling the truth. With a twist of her wrist, she pulled and tugged at his length and scrapped her nails along his tightening ball sac.

"Tell me, Mark. Tell me what you want to do to me right now."

His lips curled over his teeth, and his eyes glittered with a warning that said she was playing with fire. "I want to fuck you. I want to spread your legs wide and sink my cock balls-deep into your cunt. Happy now?"

Almost.

A shudder rolled through him as she straddled his thighs and leaned forward to whisper in his ear. "The only thing that would make me happier is if you actually put words into action and fucked me."

"Little she-devil," he grunted then slid his hand down her belly to bunch the hem of her gown in his fist. With his other hand he reached beneath her to trace along her slit with his blunt fingertip. "But that's not all I want to do to you."

"Oh, yeah?"

"Yeah." He thrust two fingers deep into her sheath, so deep she swore she felt the delicious pressure in her belly.

A scream of pleasure tore from her lips. "Man, you do that so well."

"Just wait," he murmured in her ear.

Those talented fingers began to move, massaging and stroking while his thumb circled her clit over and over. In no time her pussy fluttered and tightened with impending orgasm.

"Already, sweetheart? You're ready to come this fast?" he asked with a husky chuckle. She bit her lip and dug her fingernails into his muscled shoulders. "You are so beautiful, Gabriella. Everything about you is so sensual. I love the way you say my name. The way your breasts jiggle. How you tremble.

Everything about you I find fascinating." He speared his fingers deeper, tapping on that magical spot and pushed her closer to the edge. As she wound tighter and tighter, his labored breathing matched her own. "Watching you come is the sexiest thing on the earth. Come for me now, baby. That's it, come for me."

"Mark," she gasped and a wave of heat blossomed in her womb and radiated out in a slow ebb and flow that made her desperate for more at the same time it sated her hunger. The undulating rhythm sapped the strength from her limbs and she sagged against him, riding his hand in a silent plea for more. Like the gentleman he was, he continued, stoking the flames until her head thrashed where it lay on his shoulder. "Please," she begged. "Please."

It took but a few seconds for him to lay her on her back and roll on a condom. The weight of his big body as he settled between her thighs promised exquisite pleasure, a vow he fulfilled as he sank deep into her sheath in one thrust.

The sight of him above her, with his head thrown back, muscles tense, so strong, so powerful, sent ripples rolling through her pussy. She loved everything about the way he looked, from the way the veins bulged in his biceps as he held himself above her, to the glisten of sweat along his hairline.

Never before had she felt so decadent, so completely ravished as she allowed him to take her as he wished. Reveling in the flex of his ass under her hands as he pumped and his shaft grew harder and harder with each plunge. The head of his cock repeatedly struck the spot that he alone claimed, drawing out the pleasure to an almost painful level.

Where Mark led, she followed, willingly, breathlessly, until she leapt off the cliff with glorious abandon, falling, falling into the depths of ecstasy with her arms wide open.

"So fucking beautiful," he groaned then arched his back with a moan that seemed ripped from his soul. Hips locked tight against her as his shaft pulsated with each shot of his cum.

Time seized to exist while she was locked in his embrace. Rubber bands had more strength than her arms as she attempted to pull down on his shoulders.

"Come here, sweetie," she cooed and ran her hands up and down his sweaty back as tremors shook him.

"I'm squishing you," he muttered against her breast.

"I like it." Her voice sounded raw and husky from her cries.

"Good, because I couldn't move if I wanted to. Hell, I'd stay inside you forever, if I could. Even longer."

Post-orgasmic euphoria made it impossible to do any more than hum her approval, but her mind wandered abuzz with possibilities, while above her, Mark began to snore softly.

That was fast. She chuckled and hugged him tighter. With the tip of her finger, she traced along his eyebrow and down the side of his handsome face. At that moment she was safe, and she agreed with Mark. If she could, she'd lay there for as long as humanly possible.

Could this really be a beginning for them? As she lay there, pressed into the mattress, her heart screamed *Yes!* Yet her cautious mind warned, *Whoa girl, what's the rush?* There was still the little matter of she had no home, no livelihood, and Drew was making attempts to contact her.

She wasn't foolish enough to think that by hanging up on him, her ex-husband got the message that she wanted nothing to do with him. Somehow, some way, he was going to try to contact her again. And if he was stupid enough to show up at the ranch, could she allow Mark to fight her battle for her? With her?

No. She cuddled him closer and vowed that if Drew showed his smarmy face anywhere near her, she'd do anything to keep Mark out of her war.

Chapter Sixteen

G ABRIELLA ADJUSTED THE bodice of her dress for the umpteenth time in the last twenty minutes. She had brought the royal purple, jersey knit dress to wear for potential job interviews, but by the way the fabric clung to her full breasts and emphasized her small waist, she now wondered if perhaps she was exposing too much cleavage. This was the land of gingham and church socials, after all.

A dull throb enveloped her toes, which were encased in her three-inch Manolo Blahniks. For the last week, she'd been running around in her cowboy boots or going barefoot. Now it was difficult to believe the toe-pinching beauties had once been part of her wardrobe for so long.

Looking over her shoulder, she turned and checked out the reflection of her backside in the full-length mirror in Mark's bedroom. Visible panty line was a definite Harvest Festival no-no.

Since she had arrived at the ranch two weeks prior, she had spent a total of one night in the main house, sleeping most nights safely in Mark's arms. She still helped Greta out at breakfast when morning sickness hit her the hardest, but almost all of her belongings had made their way into his home.

She heard the shower turning off and a smile came to her

lips. All too readily, an image of Mark naked, muscular, and dripping wet came to mind. Hmmm, she could stare at that man for hours. Didn't matter what he was doing. Drinking coffee, sleeping, standing still. Holy hell, watching him on horseback made her want to tackle him to the ground and have her wicked way with him. And the best part of all was he didn't hesitate to tell her he felt the same way.

The bathroom door opened, emitting steam and revealing a tall, dark, dreamy man, wearing nothing but a towel. Her mouth went dry at the sight of all that long, lean muscle.

Mark caught her staring and stilled as his gaze roved all over her body. It pleased her to no end to see the towel twitch as he continued to look his fill.

"You are, without a doubt, the prettiest thing I've ever seen." The husky timbre in his voice made her breath catch.

"You too." She smiled then laughed when he tossed her a wink.

The towel came off and he bent over to pull some clothes from the bottom dresser drawer. An ache filled her jaws, making her want to sink her teeth into his delectable flank.

"I can feel your eyes on me," he said without turning around.

"I can't help it. Especially when you go around naked. You're just asking for trouble there, Webber."

Deep, rich laughter rumbled from his throat. Oh, she loved the way he laughed. It carried an almost surprised quality, as if he hadn't expected to find something to be funny. Not that she considered him to be without humor, but she definitely noticed how he joke and engage in conversation, but never really appeared totally relaxed while around the other hands. It wasn't until the two of them were alone that the more playful man emerged. And with each day, she fell for him harder and harder.

"Hey," she said when he pulled a dark blue shirt out of the closet. "That's not your standard black."

"I believe the sales girl called it midnight blue." He shrugged it on and worked the buttons closed.

"Is it new?"

"Yep."

She didn't remember him going shopping recently. "When did you get it?"

"The other week. I wanted to impress my new girlfriend. Looks like it worked." He tucked the tail into his jeans then straightened his cuffs.

The term he used made her pause. "Is that what I am? Your girlfriend?"

That intense light entered his eyes, sending chills over her body. "Sweetheart, I consider you to be so much more than my girlfriend. But I don't say anything because I don't want you to go all twitchy."

"I'm never twitchy," she argued and crossed her arms over her chest.

"Yes, you are. I know that until this whole issue with your ex is solved, you won't feel free." He rubbed his warm hands up and down her bare arms. "I understand, Gabriella. I do."

Damn. She hated that he was right and saw right through her. As long as Drew was out on bail, she felt as if her life were on hold.

When she had notified the detective handling her case that her ex-husband had contacted her, he worked with the judge and a date for the trial was moved up for two months from then. An improvement, but the waiting was still killing her.

"Darlin', you should know that with you, I'm thinking long term. If that's something you don't want, you should probably tell me now."

As she gazed up at his handsome face and warm eyes, she found she could deny him nothing. He treated her like a queen. Supported her, encouraged her, actually listened when she spoke. How could she even think about not seeing this through?

"I don't mind you if you call me your girlfriend."

His slow smile curled one corner of his mouth then spread to the other in a tiny glimpse before she closed her eyes and stood on her tiptoes to press her lips to his. His arms wrapped around her and pulled her close. Mark's kisses were her drug of choice, sending her to the moon with the slightest touch. A low vibration traveled from her lips down to her toes, then back up again to pool in her belly like warm buttered rum. He never rushed and always tasted every bit of her mouth. Her bottom lip, her tongue, even the soft inside of her cheek. Nothing was left wanting.

"Can't we stay in tonight?" she pleaded and skimmed her lips over the skin of his freshly shaven cheek.

He stepped back with a groan. "That's very tempting, but I want to hold you close while standing under the stars. And if we don't go, your brother is going to know why we stayed behind. Those looks he shoots me at the breakfast table are starting to get annoying."

She laughed and pulled on her shawl. "Maybe you shouldn't walk in with such a big smile on your face."

"Impossible. You make me happy."

That simple statement was the nicest compliment she ever received because she knew he didn't say it to tease. He meant it, she made him happy.

Heat burned her cheeks, and she looked down at the toe of her shoe. What does one say to something like that? Back at ya? Thank you?

I love you?

No. It was too soon to say, "I love you." For Pete's sake, they just settled on declaring themselves boyfriend and girlfriend, which was so entirely messed up. One did not have mind-blowing sex every night without feeling something akin to love. At least she didn't.

But every time she felt the urge to spill those three little words, her throat closed up tight and an ominous feeling took root in her belly. She couldn't shake the feeling that if she spoke too soon, she'd jinx them somehow and this little piece of paradise she'd found would crumble.

As if sensing her inability to respond, Mark brushed a kiss to her cheek then to her shoulder. Before he pulled away, she placed a hand on his jaw and pressed her lips directly to his, keeping her eyes open and locked on his with the hope he could see in her gaze what she was afraid to say.

Without another word he took her hand and escorted her down the stairs and to his truck. They could have hitched a ride with Trey and Greta, but Mark told her he wanted his own mode of transportation in case they wanted to leave the party early.

In the cab's cozy interior he kept her hand pressed to his thigh, his palm covering hers. Somehow, in the last minute, a shift had occurred in their relationship. As if an invisible rope drew them closer together in a way that ignited a flare of anxiety that left her trembling.

Mark was so different from Drew that she found her brain working harder to understand him which, when one thought about it, was rather ridiculous. With Mark, there was no subterfuge, no hidden meanings. You got what you saw. All during her marriage, she'd had to decipher so many subtleties and innuendoes from Drew and his peers that at times she found it difficult to accept what Mark said at face value. In her deepest of hearts, she was afraid to believe for fear of being hurt again.

A squeeze on her hand brought her attention back to his face. He flashed her a small smile before turning his attention back to the road.

Poof. And just like that, the band around her chest eased and she sighed an easy breath.

Right there was what Mark did best. He always seemed to know when she was struggling with something and let her work through it on her own with only a squeeze of her shoulder or a brief hug of support.

She drew in another breath filled with the scent of leather, spearmint, and Mark, steeping the cloud in her lungs before letting it out along with all of her apprehension. One day at a time. That was what Mark always said. Just take it one day at a time.

Martinez's Orchard was lit up like a bright starry constellation in the middle of inky blackness. Mark pulled into the designated parking lot and killed the engine while she stifled a chuckle. Never before had she seen so many pickup trucks in one location.

Ever the gentleman, Mark rushed to her side to open her door. "Ready, darlin'?"

She took his hand and was grateful for his assistance when she took two steps and almost tripped as her heels skittered across the gravel.

"Am I gonna have to carry you in?" he asked as he pushed back the brim of his hat.

"Oh God no," she gasped, feeling her cheeks heat. "Just go slow. I'll be fine."

He nodded then slid his arm around her back, taking most of her weight as they followed the crowd through the lattice archway.

"This is beautiful," Gabriella exclaimed and smiled with delight at the postcard-perfect scene before her.

Christmas lights strung amongst the apple trees created a sparkling lane, herding all of the guests to the entertainment. The spicy scents of barbecue and cinnamon wafted from the food vendors, making her stomach growl as she passed the stand of caramel apples and hot cider. Children ran past them, shrieking with joy and chasing each other with lit sparklers, while nearby a girl leapt into her boyfriend's arms, smothering him with kisses after he knocked down a pyramid of milk cans.

"Do you need me to win you a teddy bear?" Mark asked.

She loved how he didn't say "try." To him, it was a given that he could provide her with whatever she wanted. "No, I'm good. Thanks."

"Just let me know if you change your mind," he said in all seriousness.

She kissed his cheek in reply. Even his whimsy was serious.

Right in the middle of all the activity was a large dance floor. A swirl of orange caught her eye as the crowd parted, revealing Trey and Greta spinning across the floor with moves that looked as if they were in a dance competition. The skirt of Greta's pumpkin-colored dress swung with her graceful movements as Trey spun and dipped his laughing wife. Even a deaf, dumb, and blind person would be able to feel the immense love the two felt for each other. Their happiness was so blinding, it was almost difficult to watch them.

Gabriella swallowed the lump in her throat, caught up with the yearning to experience a love like that. To have someone look at her as if he couldn't imagine a world without her in it.

Mark's fingers tightened on her waist, and she looked up to see all of the hope and yearning she felt mirrored in the set of his lips and the glimmer in his eyes as his gaze was fixed on the couple. Well, to be more precise, Greta.

Gabriella recalled the story Greta told her of the—she didn't know what to call it, really—emotional affair between her and Mark, and she wondered just how deep the connection had been. Sure, the two of them could say everything was fine and they were nothing but friends now. Greta had certainly moved on with her husband, but what of Mark? Was he wishing that he was the one dancing with Greta? Even just a little bit?

Oh, jealousy was an ugly creature. Burned like acid and felt as thick as molasses as it rolled through her belly. As much as Gabriella wished she could shrug off her insecurities, the green monster had sunk its claws in deep and wasn't letting go.

"They're quite the dancers," she said, her inner radar up and ready for action.

He glanced down at her, then back at them. "Yeah, they are. The Harvest Festival is special to them. It was where they first met."

If there was ever a time that she wished she could read minds, it was at that moment. Damn, he was good at locking up his emotions in a nanosecond. The dreamy expression he had just a moment ago was replaced with one of calm. There was no tightening around his mouth or a flinch near his eyes that might indicate if he was distressed or upset. Hmmm. Maybe any lingering feelings he had toward Greta *had* changed.

And why should she care? All of that was long ago, and obviously nothing would ever come of it now. Water under the bridge and all of that other crap people tended to tell themselves to feel better about the present. She didn't care. Really.

Keep telling yourself that, sweetheart. Maybe you'll believe it.

"Mark!" a female voice called from the crowd.

A tall, willowy woman approached them, and Gabriella had to fight the compulsion to smooth her dress and check her teeth for lipstick. Straight black hair fell past the woman's shoulders left bare by her emerald green silk halter dress. The sweetheart neckline emphasized a slim and trim figure Gabriella would never be able to achieve, even if she ran hours on the treadmill and ate nothing but lettuce and cucumbers for the rest of her life.

The jealousy monster prepared to roar when she realized she knew this woman. But from where? Oh, right, this was the smiling girl from the photos in Mark's house. His sister, Melody.

Holy hell. Where had her self-esteem gone? Was she going to have to give herself a pep talk every time a beautiful woman talked to Mark? She needed to get a grip. Now.

Melody's black eyes sparkled with humor as she punched Mark in the arm. "I almost didn't recognize you, big brother. Are you actually wearing a color other than black?"

"Brat." He tugged Gabriella closer to his side. "Gabriella, this is my sister, Melody."

Gabriella held out her hand. "It's nice to finally meet you."

"You too." Melody's smile was warm and welcoming. "I've heard so much about you."

That was a surprise. "You have?"

"Well, sure. Mark is always talking about you when I call. And of course you're new in town, so everyone is buzzing about the newcomer."

"They are?" Her heart sank to her stomach. "I thought I was being so inconspicuous."

Melody rolled her eyes. "As if you could pass unnoticed. Not only are you new, but you're absolutely gorgeous. There was no way you'd stay under the radar for very long."

Mark squeezed Gabriella and smiled at her in reassurance. "It's all right, sweetheart. We're all watching out for you."

His words didn't comfort her as much as she wished. She

didn't want to be "watched out for." All she wanted was to live a nice, normal life, where she didn't have to look over her shoulder all of the time.

"Hey." Melody flicked a lock of hair over her shoulder and cast a searching glance around. "Is everyone from the ranch here?"

Mark leveled a warning glare at her. "Almost everyone. Ben and Colby stayed behind. Some of the heifers are looking like they might drop early."

"Eww." She wrinkled her nose. "Thanks for that image."

"Serves you right. Stay away from my men."

"Yeah, right. I need to go to the ladies' room. Gabriella?" She raised a brow.

Gabriella restrained a smile, recognizing the subtle command. "Sure."

"Are you certain you can walk all right?" Mark asked. The only evidence of his laughter was the light in his eyes, and the ever so slight quirk on his lips.

"I'll manage just fine." She reached up to kiss his cheek.

The smile grew wider and the brim of his hat blocked out the light when he bent to kiss her on the lips. "Hurry back."

"You'll survive," Melody huffed before she tugged Gabriella by the hand. "Oooh, cute shoes."

"Thanks."

"Are they Manolos? Where did you get them?"

"The last time I was in Vegas."

"Oh, I wish we had a better shoe selection out here," she lamented as she pulled Gabriella to an area designated for the portable toilets. "There really isn't a ladies' room out here," she confirmed.

"Ah." Gabriella nodded, sensing what was coming next. She wasn't disappointed.

"So what exactly are your intentions toward my brother?"

It appeared the Webber siblings had more in common than good looks. She started to smile, then thought better of it. "Truthfully? I don't exactly know."

Melody nodded. "Look, you seem nice. But my brother has horrible luck in the relationship department. He deserves something real."

"I know about Greta."

Her brows shot sky high. "You do?"

"Their connection is really obvious."

Melody tilted her face to the sky and shook her head. "My brother is so dense sometimes. He thinks he's so secretive." She looked back at Gabriella. "So you can see why I might be a little concerned when you show up out of nowhere and all I hear is how great you are. But you've just gotten out of a really bad relationship. How do I know that you are not using him on the rebound?"

"I understand, Melody. I do. And I have asked myself that same question a million times already. But I care for your brother, very much. You know, part of me feels very fortunate to have found someone like Mark, but the other part wishes that I had found him at a different point in time. The only thing I can do is take it one day at a time."

Melody smiled. "You've been listening to Trey."

"It's more like I've been listening to Mark, who has been listening to Trey." She laughed.

Appreciation shined in Melody's eyes as she nodded. "Thank you for your honesty."

Heat hit Gabriella's cheeks. "Thank you for watching out for Mark. He needs more than one champion. You're a good sister."

"I think we are going to become the best of friends." She threaded their arms together and marched them back toward the dance floor. "Come on. Let's find ways to torture my brother. Is Rafe around?"

Gabriella threw her head back and laughed. The throaty sound drew the attention of all the men in a thirty-foot radius.

"What's so funny?" Mark asked when they met up with him at the bar.

"Just girl talk." Gabriella smiled while Melody snickered next to her.

He looked as if he had swallowed a bullfrog and it was still jumping in his stomach, but he changed the subject. "Do you want anything to drink, Li'l Bit?"

"I'll have…" she paused as the name of a horribly pretentious cocktail came to mind and nearly crossed her lips. "A beer is fine."

"Are you sure?" he asked, noticing her hesitation.

"Yes."

"I'll have one too, brother mine," Melody chimed in.

He heaved a long-suffering sigh then winked at them.

"Gabriella, I love your shoes," Greta said as she joined them, Trey at her side.

"Thank you. You guys are fantastic dancers."

"I haven't danced like that in a long time." She accepted a glass of lemonade from Trey.

"Too long," he agreed and pressed a kiss to her forehead.

"I should have known everyone would be at the bar." Jack slapped Mark on the back. "Nice shirt there, boss."

Rafe followed, looking quite handsome in a merlot-colored western-cut shirt. When his gaze landed on Melody, he flashed a wicked smile. "Well, Ms. Webber, don't you look lovely."

"You're looking foxy yourself, Rafael."

He held out his hand. "Would you care to dance?"

"I'd love to." Melody slid her palm into his and he brought it to his lips for a lingering kiss. They both flashed smiles at Mark before they disappeared into the crowd.

"Your brother likes to live dangerously," he muttered around the neck of his beer.

"So do you," Gabriella reminded him with a caress along his jaw.

"Gabriella, you are a vision in purple." Jack slid close to her. "How about a dance?"

"Well—" Before she could say otherwise, she was whisked out on the floor. "Wow, you're quick. I think Mark wanted the first dance."

"You're probably right. However, if he wasn't smart enough to capitalize on an opportunity to hold you close, that's his loss." His hands guided her hips into a rhythm slower than the beat of the music. "Let's just slow it down a little. My leg won't last long."

"What happened?" She had noticed that he walked with a limp on occasion.

"Bull stepped on it. Crushed it so bad that I almost lost it. Six surgeries and years of physical therapy later, I'm almost as good as new. Except I can't go around hopping up and down like some of these crazies here."

He nodded to her right, and the sight there made her do a double take. Adam was hopping from one foot to the other and flapping his arms like a chicken while his date laughed and fawned like he was the Lord of the Dance. She did have to give the boy some credit. While his style was lacking, he more than made up for it with enthusiasm.

Jack started laughing. "If you tell him he can't dance, he tries harder to prove that he can. We just let it slide."

"Good to know." She glanced over Jack's shoulder to see Mark looking in their direction.

The brim of his Stetson covered his eyes, but the firm set of his mouth was a neon sign that he was not happy. She blew him a kiss and those hard lips softened and blew her a tiny kiss back. She couldn't contain a giggle at the appearance of the tiny crack in his shell.

Jack frowned at her. "What are you giggling at?"

"Mark glowering at you."

"Oh yeah. That's a laugh riot." He winked. "I think I've taunted him enough for one night. I can't fault the man for having excellent taste." The song ended and he tucked her hand into the crook of his arm and escorted her back. "It was a pleasure, sugar. And I'll want another before the night is done."

As Jack moseyed along in search of another dance partner, Mark pulled her against his side. "He took my dance."

"He said you deserved it for being slow on the uptake." She leaned close and licked his earlobe. "I'll make it up to you later."

He turned his head to murmur against her lips, "I do like the way you think."

Next to them Greta let out a mournful groan. "Oh, I can't fight that barbecue smell anymore. Let's get something to eat."

"How about you, darlin'?" Mark asked Gabriella. "Are you hungry?"

"Only for you."

"Jesus, woman. You drive me crazy. Let's go feed you." He spun her around and pushed her forward. The hard rigid of his erection pressed into her backside. "Do me a favor and keep in front of me. This is an all-ages event."

Her husky laugh earned her a nip on her shoulder. The sting of pain was totally worth it.

Gabriella didn't know if it was the festive atmosphere or the excellent company that made everything she ate taste so good. The ribs were a perfect blend of sweet and spicy, the corn was nice and buttery, and sharing a sticky caramel apple with Mark was an exercise in self control for both of them. The light in his eyes when he licked the sticky sugar off her fingers made her thighs clench and her panties damp.

It wasn't long before he dragged her out onto the dance floor and pressed her close to his firm body. A long, slow sigh released from her lips as she cuddled closer, warm and secure in his arms as they swayed from side to side.

"I love the view from up here," he rumbled low in his throat.

She glanced up to see his gaze focused on the deep line of her cleavage. "Do you now?"

"Yep. All I want to do is press my face between those heavenly mounds and enjoy."

Ever since she had encouraged him to not hold back when it came to sex, he didn't hesitate to speak his mind, which she enjoyed with immense satisfaction. As she laughed, her breasts quivered above the dress's neckline.

"Now that is fascinating." He smiled with a flash of his dimples. "I need to make you laugh more often."

The smile on her face felt as if it was stretched as wide as the state of Texas as she nuzzled his cheek and melted deeper into his embrace. This was one of those perfect moments in life that she wished would never end.

"Excuse me. May I cut in?"

Her eyes flew open and a thousand bolts of electricity shot through her limbs as she jumped with a startled yelp before she realized she had even moved. Of all the places in all the world, of course he'd find her here.

"Let me guess." The controlled scorn in Mark's tone sent a ripple of unease down her spine. She had never heard that hard, dangerous voice from him before. "This must be Drew Daws."

Chapter Seventeen

G ABRIELLA STARED AT her ex-husband, wishing with everything in her that he was just a beer and sugar–induced illusion, but of course she wasn't that lucky.

From the bottom of his Ferragamo shoes to the gold cuf-flinks at his wrists, Drew looked every inch a man with money, who came from old money, who came from even older money. Among the cowboy hats and denim, Drew stuck out like a Ferrari in a lot of old Honda's.

A lock of perfectly coiffed white blond hair hung in front of his piercing sky blue eyes, and for a moment she was struck dumb by his golden-god good looks. No question, Drew was a handsome man, and she wanted to kick herself that she had become so blinded by his image that she allowed herself to ignore his behavior. Memories of the last year of her life made her stomach heave. Her fingertips felt numb as her insides sweltered. If not for the strong band of Mark's arm around her waist, she was certain she'd collapse on the floor.

Drew leveled his most charming smile at her. "You look amazing, Gabby."

Gah! He knew how much she hated that nickname.

Lifting her chin, she dared to look him in the eye and locked her knees. "You shouldn't be here, Drew. There's a restraining order against you."

"That's what I've come to talk to you about. And since you won't talk to me on the phone, you've forced me to come to you. This has all been a misunderstanding."

"Tell that to the judge. You need to leave." Her eyes darted around, and she became painfully aware that little by little, they were drawing the attention of many of the partygoers.

"Gabby." Drew heaved a sigh and shook his head like she was a reluctant child. "You don't remember what happened. You had a lot to drink that night."

Ah, so the bastard was going to start making things up now. "I wasn't drinking. And what about the other week? When your mother's butler attacked me?"

"Again, another misunderstanding. He was only checking on your welfare and you jumped to conclusions and hurt yourself. Please, let's talk things over. Here." He reached into his pocket, pulling out two gold and diamond rings that glittered brightly in his palm. "You forgot your rings."

"Those aren't mine. Not anymore."

He drew back and sucked in a breath as if she wounded him. "You are my wife. I love you."

"No, I'm not," she bit out. Her heart beat so fast she was afraid that any minute it would jump out of her throat.

By her side, Mark didn't make a sound, but second by second his body stiffened and she felt as if she were leaning against a brick wall.

"Please, Gabby," Drew pleaded with his hand still outstretched. "I want you back."

"And I want you gone. Leave now."

Fire flashed in his eyes and his nostrils flared. "Not until we talk."

"How dare you come here, you motherfucking asshole!"

Rafe's outraged bellow preceded a flurry of activity from the right as he burst through the crowd.

Murderous intent curled his lips, and his eyes were wild with rage as he reached out in Drew's direction. Jack and Adam snagged him around the waist and shoulders before he made contact while Trey blocked him from the front.

"Jesus Christ," Adam grunted as Rafe struggled to break free. "Where's Ben when you need him?"

"You touch her again and I'll kill you!" Rafe shouted, bucking and swaying. "You hear me, Daws? I'll fucking kill you!"

Well, if they hadn't been watching before, for certain every eye at the festival was now focused on their very own live version of the world's worst reality show. The only thing missing was a dozen women shouting, "That's my baby daddy!" or "I slept with my grandpa!" to make the spectacle complete.

Gabriella buried her face in Mark's shoulder, wishing the world would swallow her whole.

"Sweetheart," Mark murmured in her ear. "I think you should see to your brother."

He was right. In this agitated state, she was the only one with the best chance to calm him down.

With one eye on her ex-husband, who watched her brother struggle with bemused fascination, she crossed behind Mark and stepped between Rafe and Trey. "Rafe. Rafe." She placed a hand on either side of his face. "Rafe! I'm right here. I'm okay."

"I won't let him hurt you, Lita." His chest heaved, and the sheen in his eyes hurt her heart.

"I know. But I need you here and not in jail." She hugged him around the waist. Under her ear his heart pounded fast and furiously.

He hugged her back, wrapping his arms around her head, shielding her from the outside world. "I love you, Lita."

"I love you too."

As Rafe shook with restrained rage, she peeked around his bicep and saw Adam taking point to their right. She turned her head and saw Jack on their left as Trey and Mark completed the wall that separated her from Drew.

Tears burned her eyes with their show of support. They had promised to look out for her and they were delivering in spades.

The scene reminded Gabriella of an old-fashioned shootout, with the good guys on one side and the bad man with the haughty glare on the other. For half a second, she expected someone to make a move and whip out a six-shooter, or at least spit a stream of tobacco at the no-goodnik's feet, but everyone remained silent and still.

Until Mark shifted his weight from one foot to the other and looped his thumb in his belt. Although she couldn't see his face, she'd bet money his expression was one of granite, with his eyes glittering with obsidian fire. His voice was low and gave no quarter as he said, "It's time you left now, Mr. Daws."

"Who the hell are you?" Drew snapped.

"I'm a good friend of Gabriella's. A very good friend." He nodded to the men surrounding her. "All of us here care about her very much. I suggest you leave peacefully. Now. The sheriff will be by in ten seconds to see what this commotion is all about, and I'll be more than happy to tell him about the restraining order you're violating."

Drew straightened his shoulders with a huff. With a perfectly manicured hand, he tugged on the sleeve of his tailored sport coat. "I'm not here to cause trouble. I only wanted to speak to my wife." Over the shoulders of the cowboys defending her, his cold blue eyes pinned her where she stood. "Call me, Gabby. I still love you." With an assessing glance at Mark, he turned and disappeared into the night.

Gabriella fought the rise of bile in her throat. The man knew nothing of love, and it sickened her to think that she had once bought his line of bullshit.

"Gabriella?"

"Lita?"

"Honey, are you all right?"

Before her eyes, shapes twisted and melted together, like crayons melting in the sun. Cotton filled her ears, muffling the murmurs of the crowd as animated conversations launched around her. Someone bumped her arm, and another pressed against her back, but she couldn't do anything more than concentrate on the air moving in and out of her lungs and the beating of her heart.

"Gabriella?"

The scent of spearmint broke through her fog.

"Gabriella." A husky burr tickled her ear.

She recognized that rumble. She liked that rumble. That rumble made her feel warm and safe.

And loved.

Her lashes felt as if they were weighted down with quarters as she blinked her vision clear.

Mark stood before her. For the first time since she met him, fear for her filled his eyes and brought the corners of his mouth down. "Tell me what you need, darlin'."

"You. I need you."

He wrapped his arm around her shoulders. "Then let's go."

"Hold on a second, Hoss." Trey stopped them. "Daws might be counting on you taking off right away. He may be waiting for you out in the parking lot, or follow you back to the ranch. Let's wait half an hour and then we'll all leave together. Adam, Jack, why don't you go check the lot?"

Mark nodded. "Good thinking."

"No, no. I don't want everyone to cut their night short," Gabriella protested. It seemed that at every turn, trouble followed.

"I'm ready to go home," Greta said with an encouraging smile. "The baby is zapping my strength."

"Come on, darlin'." Mark held out his hand. "How about one last dance?"

Dancing was the last thing she wanted to do, but she really liked the idea of being enclosed in Mark's embrace and losing herself in the rhythm of the music. His hand was warm and solid against her palm, and his arm was strong around her. The danger had passed. Trauma was averted. She was safe, and that was all that mattered.

MARK CONCENTRATED ON not squishing the stuffing out of the woman in his arms. Holding her close in the middle of the dance floor was more for his benefit than hers. For one, he had absolute confirmation she was safe. Second, dancing with her prevented him from doing what he really wanted, which was to kick the shit out of the arrogant ass of her ex-husband.

Despite the dulcet melody of the Patsy Cline classic drifting from the sound system, adrenaline raced through his blood, caused not only by the urge to fight but also by pride over the courage Gabriella displayed when standing up to her ex. Damn, she had been so regal, so in control, he thought he was looking at royalty. He had been afraid for her and so turned on his teeth ached. Unfortunately, his favorite outlet to release all of that pent-up energy was Gabriella's succulent body, and with every shuffling step her curves pressed against him, heating him, enticing him, reminding him of what awaited them when they were alone in his bed.

"Hey, man." Rafe clapped him on the shoulder. "The coast is clear."

About fucking time. "Thanks. Ready to go, darlin'?"

"Ready." Her smile trembled, but she took his hand without hesitation and gripped him tight.

When they reached the gravel lot, he swung her up in his arms, not trusting her fancy heels to keep her from falling. He half expected her to put up a fuss, but when she laid her head on his shoulder, it was he whose knees threatened to buckle.

Gabriella's trust in him set off the caveman instinct that lay in wait inside him. It was him she placed her faith in. His arms she sought for comfort. He wanted to shout out to the world that this was his woman. His to protect and love. To mark as his.

And thanks to that fucker, Drew Daws, he couldn't. At least not in the way he wanted.

Daws used physical force to try to dominate Gabriella. He tried to strong-arm her into becoming someone she wasn't and turned abusive when she refused.

Mark too wanted to physically dominate her, but in a completely different manner. He wanted her to willingly give him the control. He wanted her to trust that he always keep her safe, no matter how hard he pushed her. Up until recently, she'd responded so beautifully to his strength, at times even asking for more. But now, would she react the same way? Or would memories of her past make her shy away from the animalistic couplings he'd come to crave? Whatever Gabriella needed of him, it was hers, but to hold back was going to take a herculean effort on his part.

Of course, it would be a lot easier to not think of wild and crazy sex if she wasn't plastered to his side on the front seat of his truck. As they bounced along the road, her head rested on his shoulder and her hand massaged his thigh. In order to sit next to him, she had to straddle the gearbox, which caused the skirt of her dress to hike up and expose the creamy expanse of her legs. At that moment he'd do anything to replace that haunted look in her eyes with one of pleasure, but now was not the time, and if he wasn't careful, he was going to put them in the ditch.

The sight of the Sprawling A's entrance was never before such a welcomed sight, and the fact that no strange cars littered the driveway was a bonus.

Mark parked the truck into the space alongside his house then rushed to open her door. Jack pulled up behind them and rolled down his window while Rafe jumped out of the passenger side.

"I'm going to get on Blackjack and do a quick tour of the property," he said.

"You don't have to, Rafe," Gabriella replied and hugged her arms with a shiver. "Besides, it's late. You won't be able to see two feet in front of you in the dark."

"Blackjack can see in anything, better than being on a bike or ATV. And I won't be able to sleep unless I do some scouting. I'll be all right." He embraced her tight. Over her head he met Mark's gaze and mouthed, "Thank you."

Mark nodded.

She brushed a kiss to her brother's cheek. "Be careful."

"I will." Setting her away, he headed off toward the barn.

"Good night, you two," Jack called from the truck.

"Thank you, Jack," she said.

His wide smile was a white slash in the night. "Anytime, sweetheart." He took off with a laugh.

From two different directions came the sound of footsteps crunching on the gravel. Mark shifted his weight to the balls of his feet and pulled Gabriella behind him. Trey emerged from the shadows on the right the same time Ben stepped out from the left.

"I thought I heard the sound of trucks." Ben stuffed the handkerchief he held in his back pocket. Despite the chill in the air, sweat beaded his brow and upper lip. "How was the festival?"

"Interesting," Trey answered. "How did it go here?"

"You are the owner of three new bulls. Found them on the east forty near the creek. It's weird how they decided to drop 'em at once, like they scheduled a birthing party."

"Excellent."

Ben's smile dimmed. "We did lose a fourth. Leg broke on the way out and she got caught in the cord. But Colby was able to save the mother."

Trey cursed. "That's a shame. I'm glad Colby was there."

"Me too." Ben sighed. "I sent him back to the house to rest. I think we're done for the night, but I'll take first watch."

"Hopefully tomorrow will be uneventful with all of us there to catch, if needed," Mark added.

"Yeah," Ben agreed. "Did I just see Rafe go out on horseback?"

"Why am I not surprised?" Trey started to head toward the barn. "Let's go check out my new mommy makers, and I'll fill you in. Good night, y'all," he called back to them.

"Good night." Mark guided Gabriella to his front door. "Come on. Let's get you out of the cold."

Old habits had him immediately turning the doorknob, but when it refused to budge he remembered he had taken to locking the door when Gabriella began to stay the night. She couldn't believe there was a place on Earth safe enough to go without locking your doors, and she wouldn't rest until he secured all entrances. Good thing he had. All he needed was to walk in and find Daws sitting in his living room.

Mark ushered her into the house and locked the door behind them. "Why don't you go upstairs and get ready for bed? I'll be up in a minute."

"Mark." She tugged his hand. "What's wrong?"

"Nothing. Why?"

"You've been quieter than normal. Which scares me. Did I not handle Drew's appearance well?"

"What?" How could she even think that? "Darlin', you were fantastic. You were so calm and strong. I was so proud of you."

Delight sparkled in her eyes. "You were?"

"Hell, yeah. You were amazing and so sexy—" he broke off at the admission.

She tilted her head and squinted at him. "You thought I was sexy?"

"Darlin', I think there is nothing sexier than a strong woman."

"Really." She drew out the word and pressed against him with her soft curves. "Then why this wall between us?"

"Gabriella," he warned as he threw his hand up, halting her progression. "Look, I'm a little on edge right now. I've been hot for you all night long, and between Jack snatching you from me and Daws showing up, I'm, well, I'm horny. You're my girl, and to have another man try to lay claim on you makes me crazy. All I want to do is fuck. Fuck you hard, and often. But I don't want to scare you. So you gotta give me time to cool off. All right?"

"Ahh." She nodded. "So this is one of those moments when you think I won't be able to handle your passion?"

"This isn't funny, Gabriella."

"Am I laughing?" She set her hands on her hips and stood toe to toe with him. "Mark, you are not Drew. I know that. I've told you before. I want *you*. Not a watered-down version of you."

"Darlin', you have no idea what you wanna unleash."

A devilish smile curved her lips and the sight made his heart pound. "I do. And I want you," she whispered against his mouth then snagged him by the belt buckle and dragged him up the stairs.

Like a fool, he didn't fight. He wanted her so bad. Every inch of his body throbbed in anticipation of sinking inside her.

She stopped in the center of the bedroom and reached for the hem of her dress and lifted it up. There was a slight *pop* as the waistband cleared her voluminous breasts and then the dress was over her head and floating to the floor.

"Jiminy, Gabriella." His vision blurred and he felt unable to form an intelligent sentence. Behind his fly, his cock jerked at the sight of her standing there so proud in her sheer undergarments. Her large beaded nipples were smashed against the mesh cups of her bra and the slit of her pussy begged to be stroked through the gauzy material. "Please tell me this is what you want."

"Of course this is what I want. Now you tell me. What do *you* want?"

"Sit on the bed. Just like you are."

She sat primly on the bed and cupped her breasts, deepening the valley of her cleavage. "Would you like me to leave my shoes on?"

"Oh yeah."

Pop. Pop. Pop. He whipped the snaps of his shirt open then tossed the dark blue fabric to the floor. As the hiss of his belt sliding through the loops rippled in the air, she wet her lips as if she could already taste his skin. He almost wept with relief when his cock finally bounced free of its confines. With the shaft pointing straight in the air, he gripped the base and squeezed hard.

"Hmmm, Mark." She sighed and parted her legs. "Please let me suck you."

Happy to oblige. He stepped between her splayed thighs and offered her his cock. With one dainty hand she stroked the thick length while the other massaged his sac. He had begun to keep the hair down there trimmed like those city boys do, and loved the sensation of her fingernails on his skin.

With a lusty moan, she devoured the head of his cock and instantly his balls drew up and his eyes closed in pleasure.

No, no, no, no. He snapped his head forward, not wanting to miss a second of watching those full lips sliding up and down the veiny shaft. A groan lodged in his throat, and his fingers bit into his sides as he restrained the urge to grab her by the hair and hold her still for his thrusts.

"You taste so good," she purred and curled her tongue under the shaft.

"Baby. You gotta stop," he wheezed. "I'm gonna come."

"Come in my mouth."

His hips jerked and he bit back a curse. Sweat trickled down his back. "I want to come in your pussy more, but first I want to eat you out."

In seconds he had her bra off and pushed her flat on her back. He dropped a pillow at his feet and kneeled to worship at the altar of Gabriella. He draped her legs over his shoulders and parted her dripping lips with his thumb. *Heaven, pure heaven*, he thought and fell on her, driving his tongue deep.

"Ah, Mark," she screamed and arched her back. She palmed her tits, pulling hard on the pink tips.

Damn, he loved when she touched herself. While his eyes feasted on the wanton display, he circled her clit over and over with the tip of his tongue in the rhythm that made her gush into his mouth. In the last few weeks, he'd spent hours learning her body and knew exactly where to touch, how hard or softly to stroke to send her to the stars.

The farther he pushed her, the more fevered her cries. Up and down he strung her along, listening to the music of her passion until her pussy fluttered against his tongue for the third time, and then he knew she was ready. He crawled up her body, smearing her cream along her torso and between her breasts as he paused to place wet kisses while she caught her breath.

Scooping her under her shoulders, he sat up on his knees. "Climb on me."

"Let me. Grab a condom," she panted.

"No, no condom." She froze then turned to stare at him with wide eyes. "Nothing between us, baby. Just you and me. You're the one that I want."

Her throat worked as she swallowed hard and he swore he could sense her brain struggle through the sex-induced fog to comprehend exactly what he was asking. The throbbing column of his cock jutted angrily from his body, shouting for release, desperate to pull her on top of him, but he waited. This had to be Gabriella's choice.

Instead of answering, she placed a kiss on his lips that was so soft, sweet, he was about ready to cry with the effort to hold back and not crush her in his arms. Her hands were hot against his shoulders and the insides of her thighs slick as she straddled his quadriceps and settled over his erection. Notching the head against her opening, she sank down until she was fully seated on his thighs.

"Fuck!" he shouted. His heart was going to explode, he knew it. "Sorry. You're just so tight, and hot, and wet, and fuck, you're tight." Why did he go so long without feeling every inch of her sheath stretched snug around him?

"Mark," she gasped and braced her feet on the bed to move

her hips up and down. His name became a chant as she rode him, her clit striking the base of his cock on every stroke.

He gripped the flesh of her ass in his palms and bucked up, driving deep, so deep. Yes. He knew by her shouts that he was striking her g-spot. That spot just in front of her cervix that made her wild and hungry.

"That's it, baby. Ride me," he encouraged. "You feel so good. You're so fucking beautiful."

In his arms, she was sin and passion incarnate as she rode him like her own personal joy ride. With a strangled groan, she gripped the hair at the nape of his neck and pulled back, baring the column of his neck. She latched on, nipping the veins straining under the pressure his racing heart was putting on his body.

The scrape of her teeth ignited the final fuse in the explosion gathering in his groin. "I'm going to come inside you, Gabriella. So deep. So fucking deep."

His need to mark her and the bounce of her breasts were too powerful to ignore. Sucking a nipple into his mouth, he drew hard, his teeth latching on. The ends of her hair tickled his knees as she arched into him and screamed his name. Her pussy contracted her, stealing his breath, then pulsed wildly. Her juices drenched his thighs.

The suction was too great to fight anymore and he thrust deep, shooting his cum hard and hot inside her. He roared with each pulse that bathed the neck of her womb. When every drop was rung from his cock, he toppled over with her legs locked around his waist. His lungs burned and sweat covered them, making it difficult to hold on to her slippery form.

From out of nowhere, a wave of exhaustion swamped over him, drawing him into the dark abyss. Unable to resist the pull, he passed out with her name on his lips.

GABRIELLA CHUCKLED AND cradled Mark's head to her heaving breast. She wasn't surprised he passed out after that workout session. Sleep wasn't far from claiming her as well.

Her muscles trembled with the last of her orgasm and her pussy continued to pulse around Mark's softening cock. Even now the heat of cum he'd shot deep inside her pooled in her pussy in the most delicious sensation ever.

The only other man she let come inside her was Drew. The significance of that decision was not lost on her.

When Mark said he wanted nothing between them, she wanted to say no. It was on the tip of her tongue to say no. To go bareback would make a definitive statement that they had moved on to the next step in their relationship. A more permanent step she wasn't sure she was ready to take. But as she looked into his eyes, she knew she could deny him nothing. She loved him. It was that simple.

She loved Mark Webber.

Loved. Was that even the right word to describe how she felt for the big, silent man in her embrace?

In the beginning of her marriage to Drew, she had cared for him, even believed she loved him, but what she felt for Mark went so far beyond that. He touched her so deep in her soul, she knew her view of the world had been changed forever.

And with that realization, fear hit her dead in the gut and stole her breath. If Mark knew just how much she loved him, he'd have the power to destroy her. When her marriage to Drew ended, she was able to move on with ease because she had never really given him her heart. But Mark, oh, if Mark hurt her…the outcome was too painful to contemplate.

Of course, Mark vowed to never hurt her, and she knew he

meant it. He would never lay an unkind hand upon her, but emotionally, no one knew what the future would bring.

No, for her protection, she'd have to keep her feelings to herself. There was no way he could learn just how much she loved him. Never.

Chapter Eighteen

"THANK YOU, MR. Petri. I'll see you then." Gabriella ended the call then looked down at the phone in her hand and stifled the urge to squeal with delight.

Mark was asleep upstairs after spending all night tracking and tagging the new calves, and she didn't want to wake him. So instead of hooting and hollering, she did a silent dance of joy around the couch.

She got a job. After weeks of searching and interviews, she finally landed a job. The last of her cash was running out, and she hated borrowing gas money from Rafe and Mark. Especially Mark. The only reason she accepted the new cell phone he gave her was because he didn't want her out and about without a means to call for help if she needed it. Some women might like to be cared for financially, but her recent experiences had taught her that nothing was more important than financial freedom.

With a skip in her step, she hopped into the kitchen to finish the shopping list for her part of the Thanksgiving feast that was to be held at the Armstrongs. She now had lots to be thankful for with a new job, a great boyfriend, and no sign of Drew Daws.

His surprise appearance at the Harvest Festival was the last she had seen of the creep, but apparently he'd been blowing up her lawyer's phone line with the same sob story. He wanted her back. She'd misunderstood him, yadda, yadda, and more bullshit. In a few weeks, the trial would be under way and soon he'd be nothing but a bad chapter in her past.

"A smiling, beautiful, and barefoot woman in my kitchen. How did I get so lucky?"

She glanced over her shoulder to where Mark stood leaning against the doorframe, looking all sexy with his thick hair stuck up around his head and stubble on his chin. A pair of jeans hung low on his hips, leaving a gorgeous display of toned male torso for her eyes to feast upon.

Talk about being lucky. She leaned against the counter and let out a long slow breath, appreciating the masculine beauty that was Mark. Under her lingering gaze, his chest rose and fell with his quickening breath, and he sucked in his abs while the bulge under his fly swelled. To know that just a look from her affected him so was a heady sensation, and her thighs quivered with the need to ride him for as long as her legs could support her.

A smile flitted on his lips. Oh, yeah, he knew the feelings were more than mutual. He stood there, as still as could be, and let her look her fill. "What has you in such a good mood?"

Besides you? "I got a job."

"Really?" He straightened, and the sensual fog around them snapped and dissipated like a million tiny bubbles. "Which one?"

"I am the new events planner at the Ponderosa Pines Golf Club," she announced with a ramrod-straight posture and her hands on her hips.

"That's great, sweetheart." Those dimples came out with his wide smile. He swiftly crossed the kitchen in his own bare feet to swing her up into a hug. "They'd have been fools not to snatch you up."

One of the many things she loved about him was his unwavering faith in her and her abilities.

She pressed her nose into his chest and inhaled his sleepy, manly scent. She grew dizzy on the exhale as her senses spun. With her lips against his neck, she murmured into his skin, "Now I can pay you back for the cell phone."

"Absolutely not. Besides, you've already paid me back." He slid his hands down to cup her ass, lifting her into the crook of his groin. "Repeatedly."

His mouth captured hers in a hungry kiss and as his lips rubbed against hers with demand, she answered by parting for the sweep of his tongue. All along his front, she wiggled and squirmed, molding to his hard frame.

His teeth caught her lower lip and tugged before he pulled away and let it go. He licked at the mark. "Let's go celebrate."

She smiled and nibbled along his jaw line. "You want me to spend money before I earn it?"

"You're not spending nothing. This is my treat. We'll go someplace real nice for dinner, like in Yakima. Maybe get a room, spend the night. Play kinky games."

"Oooh." She raked her nails over his pectoral muscles. "You mean we could pretend not to know each other and you pick me up at a bar?"

He jerked at the touch. "Maybe. I could try to seduce you to have sex with me on the first date."

"You know, we did have sex the first day we met," she reminded him.

"No. It was the second."

"How ever did we hold out for so long?" She nipped his shoulder.

"Unbelievable self control." His easy smile warmed her heart and heated her blood. "Hey, I have the perfect congratulations present."

He pulled her into the living room then opened the drawer to the old secretary desk that had belonged to his great-grandmother. When he turned around, a silver box sat on his palm.

For half a second, visions of Mark dropping to his knees struck her dumb, but then she realized the box was the wrong size for a ring. As her heart rate returned to normal, she glanced up and smiled at the twinkle in his eyes and his boyish grin.

The box was light in her hands, and when she lifted the lid, a pair of ruby red, teardrop earrings winked at her from a pillow of cotton. A pair of earrings that looked awfully familiar.

"Are these for me?" She frowned up at him in confusion.

He laughed. "Well, yeah. They're not for me."

"Oh. These look like a pair I've seen Greta wear."

"She made them for me. I thought they'd go well with your red dress."

"I don't have a red dress."

"You don't?" He blinked. When she shook her head, he shrugged. "I thought you did. Well, maybe I'll get you one tonight."

"They're lovely. Thank you." She kissed his cheek then set the opened box on the shelf. An odd rolling sensation settled in her stomach as the beads looked back at her as if they were the eyes of a snake.

A second later her world turned upside as he flipped her up and over his shoulder and headed up the stairs.

"Mark!" she squeaked, latching onto his back pockets. "What are you doing?"

"Carrying you upstairs. You made my cock hard and now I want to fuck you." He set her on her feet next to the bed. "You have a problem with that?"

The dark flush on his cheeks and his heavy breathing fueled

the hunger inside her. She needed to taste and touch and push him to the point where he forgot to be gentle and took her hard and deep.

She ran her thumb around his navel, enjoying the brief flare of his nostrils. "I have one thing I need to do first."

"What's that?" His voice dropped so low it vibrated down her arm and teased her nipples.

"Make you scream." She stood on her tiptoes to dip her tongue in the dimple that formed in his cheeks as he smiled at her bold words.

"Baby, I don't scream. I may shout, even holler, but never will I scream."

"Challenge accepted."

It didn't take much cajoling to push him onto the bed. She hiked her short denim skirt up to her hips to allow her the freedom to straddle his waist. The sensation of his jeans rubbing against the insides of her bare thighs was a delicious promise. Palm to palm, she linked their fingers together and positioned them over his head while she devoured his mouth in a deep, drugging kiss that sent fire straight to her pussy. She ground her groin against the thick ridge trapped in his jeans, inhaling the groan that welled from his throat.

She wrenched away to draw air into her burning lungs. "Don't move," she panted in warning before dropping kisses over his collarbone and down his sternum.

She laved his nipples with her tongue, nibbling them until they formed tiny red peaks. The scar on his side from an unfortunate encounter with barbed wire received the same wet treatment, as well as the scar on his belly from when he crashed his dirt bike into a tree as a teenager.

She pressed her smile into the skin above his waistband. Every muscle in his body went tight as she worked the button-fly open. She licked her lips in anticipation as his cock sprung free. A hot column of flesh, and all hers to play with.

Mark struggled upright, his hands pressed flat to the mattress to support his upper body.

"I told you to stay down." With both hands she gripped his cock then paused, enjoying the pulse of his flesh in her palms.

"I want to watch you put your mouth on me." His eyes glazed over as she began to stroke his length, hand over hand, in firm movements.

He held his breath as she hovered over the already drooling tip. Gazing into his wide eyes, she took him deep into her mouth, going down as far as she could go before she gagged. There was no pause, no relief for him as she worked her mouth up and down, hollowing her cheeks to suck him harder.

His eyes rolled and he alternated between moans and panting, curses and groans that seemed pulled deep from his soul. He bunched the quilt in his hands, crushing it in his fists as his body quaked.

Her pussy melted, cream dampened her panties as she suckled him, tasted him. Her tongue never stopped moving, pressing firmly against the veins that ran up the underside of the heavy shaft. Each second he swelled more, tightened, as pre-cum coated her tongue, telling her he was losing control.

She pulled away with a long lick. "If I let you come in my mouth, will you still have the energy to fuck me?" she questioned with her wickedest smile.

His lips curled back. "Bring it on, baby."

She went back to work with a laugh. She let her teeth scrape ever so gently along his length as she moved one hand to curl under his tight ball sac to rub and fondle.

The breath burst from his lungs and his groan turned into a wail. "God, that's good." He fell back on the mattress. "You're a fantasy come true, Greta."

Chapter Nineteen

S OMETHING WAS WRONG. At the moment he didn't even know his own name, but he at least had the brainpower to recognize something was most definitely wrong.

One minute he was in heaven with his cock buried deep in the throat of the woman he loved and on the verge of an orgasm to end all orgasms. Then all of a sudden it was as if an ice-cold blanket was tossed over his hot shaking body.

"Wha–what?" he mumbled with a shake of his head. His vision blurred, then cleared like a camera lens trying to focus.

Gabriella stood by the side of the bed. The flush on her cheeks had drained to a sickly white and her brown eyes were like two shimmering pools filled with disbelief and hurt.

The climb to coherence was slow and arduous, and his voice rasped. "What's wrong, Gret—"

Their eyes widened at the same time.

Fuuuuck.

Bam! The girl was gone before the word "jackass" stopped echoing in his brain. On the stairs, the pounding of her footfalls beat an ominous warning that his troubles had just begun.

"Wait! Sweetheart! I didn't mean it. Damn it."

Fear-based adrenaline raced through his veins, making the room sway and his limbs feel as if they were hog-tied. He made a half-assed attempt at stuffing his now-flaccid cock back into his jeans and flew down the stairs, jumping the last three steps in one leap.

"Please, baby. I didn't mean it." He managed to wedge himself between her and the door. "I'm sorry."

"I can't believe I fell for it." She sucked in a breath. Tears hovered on the edge of her eyelashes. "Get out of my way."

"No, I swear it was a mistake." A horrible, horrible mistake.

"Right. You know, I'm sure you dropped to your knees and praised the Lord when stupid me fell in your lap. The perfect idiot to mold into a version of her!"

"What are you talking about?"

"Did you think I didn't know Greta was the woman you were in love with? That it was Greta you wanted for so long? I am not her!"

The roar of his blood muffled his hearing. "I—I don't—I never—"

"Oh, please. How many times have I heard you say in the past few weeks, 'You and Greta have so much in common.' 'You're such a great cook. Just like Greta.' 'You look like sisters.'"

"That's insane." Her accusation slammed into his gut with the force of a ten-ton bull. The idea was too twisted to comprehend.

"Get out of my way."

"No. Not until you talk to me rationally."

A wild light turned her eyes molten gold as the skin over her cheeks tightened. He swore her hair swirled around her head as if blown by an invisible wind.

"I am completely rational." She reached for one of the books on the shelf next to her shoulder. "Now. Get. Out. Of. My. Way!" Each word was punctuated by a book thrown in his direction.

"Dammit. Stop." He dodged left, then right. A thick volume of the *Farmer's Almanac* caught him in the shin. "Ow!"

"Here's a pair of earrings that look exactly like hers." She withdrew the silver box from the shelf and let it fly. "They go great with the red dress you don't have, but I bet Greta does." A candlestick holder left a good-sized dent in the wall behind him. "We are so done."

The one-two punch of the remote control aimed at his groin and the book hitting his shoulder distracted him enough for her to slip past him and dash out the door.

With each step she ran away from him, he felt the tie of their bond weakening. "Darlin', please."

"My name is Gabriella." She turned on him. "Not darlin', not sweetheart, not baby and for hell's certain not Greta. It's Gabriella." She jerked her chin up. "Ms. Montoya to you," she trilled in that accent that made his cock twitch even as his stomach filled with dread.

"Gabriella," he pleaded. He reached out a hand and barely brushed her arm as she ran down the stairs.

"Don't touch me!" she screamed.

She bent down and picked up a rock the size of her fist. She hurled it with all of her might straight at his head. The stone whirled past his ear and hit the doorframe, making a sizable dent in the wood.

As regal as a queen, she marched down the road, not even flinching as dirt and gravel bit into her bare feet.

Mark stood on the porch, frozen in place and dizzy with shock. He thought he'd seen all of her moods. Joy, fear, sexy, sad. But this burning, passionate betrayal blew him away. It absolutely gutted him.

In the distance he heard a door slam, not once, but twice.

Confirmation. She was beyond pissed, and it was all his fault.

The wind kicked up and despite his being shirtless, the cold didn't affect him as his entire body went numb.

She had bet she could make him scream, and he was. On the inside, his heart was screaming for him to go after his woman and make things right, but in the state of mind she currently was in, she was more likely to seriously maim one or both of them, and odds were it would be him on the floor bleeding. He had made a vow to give her whatever she wanted, and at that moment it was obvious she wanted time. It killed him to be apart from her when she was in so much pain, but he could at least grant her a few hours to settle down.

He shuffled back into the house and closed the door behind him with a gentle nudge. At his feet lay the silver jewelry box. The earrings had spilled out and were scattered across the floor like drops of blood. A sharp pain raced up his chest as his heart beat out a frantic rhythm. Her accusations rang in his ears, and his legs gave out, sending him to the floor with only the door at his back for support.

She had actually thought he was using her, molding her, as a replacement for Greta. Seriously? And here he thought he'd done everything in his power to show her how much he loved her. *Her.* But apparently all she heard was how she measured up to Greta.

Was she right?

Had he subconsciously imposed his former feelings for Greta on Gabriella?

No. No, of course not. While his best friend's wife had certain characteristics that were similar, the two were completely different. Greta was campfires and warm fuzzies, a spring rain and hot toddies, while Gabriella was an illegal bonfire and salsa dancing, tornadoes, and Fireball whiskey.

Gabriella lit him up in ways he didn't think were possible. She was his match.

Bile rose in his throat as he recalled the look in her eyes when he began to call her the wrong name. The expression on her face made it look as if he'd slapped her. With one careless word, he'd damaged her trust. Maybe to the point of never being repaired.

"What have I done?" he muttered. His knees came up and he curled into a ball.

Somehow, some way, he was going to have to make her believe him. Whatever it took to get her trust back, he'd do. Even if he had to cut his heart out and hand it to her. Anything.

GABRIELLA CAME TO a halt in the middle of the mudroom. All of the rage and hurt she had yet to work out bubbled up and exploded like a rocket.

"Motherfucking asshole!" she screamed at the top of her lungs. The force of her cry doubled her over and nearly brought her to her knees.

A shadow fell over her and when she looked up, the second to last person on Earth she wanted to see stood in the doorway, ladle in hand.

"Gabriella?" Greta asked. "What's wrong?"

"Not now, Greta." She moved past her and through the kitchen.

"Wait! What happened? Is it Drew? Is he back?" She followed after her down the hall.

"Not now, Greta," she gritted between clenched teeth.

"Gabriella, please. You are obviously upset. What happened?" She caught her by the hand.

Gabriella whirled around with one foot on the bottom stair.

The limit on her patience was now officially blown all to hell. "I was giving Mark a blow job, and he called me by your name."

Clack. The ladle hit the floor, splashing gravy over their feet. Yeah, Gabriella thought that might get her to back away.

Greta's lashes fluttered and her mouth opened and closed. She couldn't have looked more stunned if Gabriella had turned blue and twisted her head all the way around.

"That fucking idiot," Greta breathed out vehemently.

Whoa. Now it was Gabriella's turn to blink in surprise. She'd never heard Greta swear. Aside from the occasional *damn*. While her use of the expletive did make Gabriella feel better, slightly, she was light years away from feeling relaxed and groovy.

Without another word, Gabriella raced up the stairs to her former room. Her hands itched to cause more destruction, but the only items at hand didn't belong to her.

"Fuck, fuck, fuck." The tears she held in check breached her lashes and fell down her cheeks in hot streams.

She rushed to the bathroom and splashed cold water on her face. "Stop it. Stop it." She refused to cry over another man.

"Gabriella?" There was a knock at the bedroom door before Greta poked her head in.

She dropped her head deeper into the sink. "I would like to be alone, please."

"I know, I'm probably the last person you want to see right now, but I need to talk to you. Gabriella, you have to know that I'm really sorry."

"Why are you sorry?" The ends of the towel snapped with her irritation as she dried her face. "Did you sleep with him?"

Greta's eyes bulged as she sputtered. "No!"

"Do you want to?"

A ripple of horror shook her shoulders. "Of course not."

"Then you have nothing to be sorry for. It's all the asshole's fault." She was pissed, not unreasonable.

The bed frame rattled as she flounced onto the mattress. With the damp towel she swiped at the dirt covering her feet.

"Look, Gabriella, you have every right to be angry. And I cannot even begin to imagine what was going through his head when he said what he did. But I know that he must be feeling just awful about it." She threw up her hands at the quelling look Gabriella shot her. "And he should. What he did was inexcusable."

When Gabriella refused to respond, Greta sat at the foot of the bed. "Gabriella, he loves you. You have to know that. I've never seen him look at a woman the way he looks at you. No one. Not even me. You make him smile. You make him laugh. It's you he loves. I'm sure it wasn't on purpose. Just give him a chance."

"I gave another man a second chance and he beat me," she shot back, then instantly regretted it.

Greta's nostrils flared. "That's not the same."

No, it wasn't. In a way, this was worse.

Gabriella wanted to forgive Mark. Pretend that it didn't happen. But Greta didn't know. Greta hadn't felt the burning stab of betrayal rip through her gut when the man she loved, the man writhing and panting from the pleasure she was giving him, call her by another's name. Another woman she saw every day. A woman he had once given his heart to.

"I'm not going to allow him to hurt me again." The finality of her tone hung in the air as she rose and crossed to the closet.

"It's the ones that we love that we hurt the most with our own thoughtlessness."

Tears burned her eyes again at Greta's words, but she blinked them away. "Fool me once, and all that shit. Not happening again."

She flung the closet doors open and rummaged through the clothes she had left behind. To Mark's home she had moved all of her new, country clothes, not having any use for her slacks and dresses. These were the clothes of the wife of a lawyer. Upscale outfits meant to create an image. An image of style and confidence that she needed more than ever right at that moment. From the corner of her eye, she spotted a pair of strappy, pink-jeweled Ferragamos. Excellent.

She switched out her T-shirt for a silky magenta blouse and strapped the flashy stilettos for a bit of sparkle. Her arches promptly cramped from having gotten used to running around flat-footed for the past month. She bounced on the balls of her feet to warm up the muscles, then reached for her clutch. Looking in the mirror, she slicked pink lip gloss over her lips then used her fingers to work the worst of the tangles from her hair. Her lips were still swollen from Mark's kisses, giving her a sexy pouty look that begged for male attention.

"Gabriella, I don't like that look in your eye. What are you planning?"

"I'm going out." She adjusted the strap of her purse across her body and twirled the keys in her hand, creating a festive jingle.

Greta got to her feet. "I don't think that's a good idea. Stay here. Wait an hour or so, and then talk things out with Mark."

A growl slipped past her lips before she could stop it. She knew Greta was only trying to help, but she desperately needed to be anywhere outside a ten-mile radius of Mark and Greta.

"I need to go, Greta. If you are really my friend, you will understand why. And you will not tell Mark anything." She sliced her hand through the air when Greta made to protest. "It's the least you can do."

Greta snapped her mouth shut and nodded. "Can you tell me where you're going? Otherwise, I'm going to worry about you."

"Mark and I had made plans to go out and have a good time tonight. And I'm still planning to."

Chapter Twenty

THE CRESCENT MOON bar was moderately full for a Thursday evening, and Gabriella was fresh meat to the men who came in for an after-work beer. She felt their stares roam all over her body, but it appeared as if she intimidated these cowboys. They watched her from afar and anonymously sent drinks her way, yet none were bold enough to make a move.

Until that moment.

"Darling, that sweet ass of yours is just asking for trouble."

Hmm, now which cowhand had finally gathered the courage to hit on her?

She glanced over her shoulder and her lips stretched into a delighted smile. "Jack," she drawled out. "What a pleasant surprise."

She turned around and leaned with her back against the bar. The motion thrust out her full breasts, straining the buttons that ran down the front and exposing a good portion of her lacy bra between the gap of the buttons. She took her time drinking in the sight of the ranch hand's well-muscled chest molded against the tight white T-shirt under his denim jacket and his long legs encased in well-worn jeans. The man was quite scrumptious.

Something in her demeanor must have set off a warning, for his eyes narrowed with suspicion before his blue gaze swept the room. "Where's Mark?"

"Don't know." She shrugged. "Don't care."

His brow rose and he sucked in a slow breath then just as slowly let it out. He swaggered closer and copied her slump against the bar. "What did he do?"

She turned back to her drink and rimmed the lip of her glass with her fingertip. "What do you mean?"

"Sweetheart, you are at the Crescent Moon, by yourself, in a short skirt and fuck-me shoes. There is no way Mark let you out of the house looking like sin in heels. What did he do?"

"I don't want to talk about Mark. I came here to have a good time."

"And if you're not careful, you're going to have a lot of offers for more than you can handle."

"Please," she snorted. "You're the first man to actually approach me all night."

"That's because they all know you belong to Mark and think he's here. Once they realize different, they'll be on you like flies on honey."

"I don't belong to Mark," she snapped.

"Darling, you and I both know Mark claimed you from day one."

And he had. From the moment he first smiled at her, she was his.

She shook her head. "Not anymore."

"What did he do?"

Damn it. Didn't these people know when to let it go? She clenched her teeth and swung her gaze up to look him in the eye. "He called me by another woman's name while we were intimate."

His mouth fell open into a silent "o." After a few moments, he scratched his head then leaned over the bar to wave two fingers at the bartender before turning back to her.

"Well. You have to hand it to the man. When he fucks up, he does it big." He pushed the fresh beer in front of her. "I'm sorry, honey."

She shrugged and took a long swallow. The cold liquid mixed with the tears burning the back of her throat, creating an elixir of sorrow. "What brings you out here?" she asked in an attempt to change the subject.

"I need to get the stench of cattle out of my nose on occasion." He flashed her his trademark smile. "Finding you here was a lovely bonus."

The white of his teeth set off a flutter in her tummy. "Do you have a girlfriend, Jack?"

"Nope."

"Ever been in love?"

He frowned in thought. "Not that I remember."

Perfect.

She leaned into his side, until her breasts rested on his arm. "I'm glad I ran into you tonight, Jack."

The corner of his lip curled up. "And you, my dear, are playing with fire. Are you trying to get me killed?"

"Who would want you dead?"

"Rafe, for one. And when he was done, Mark would make sure I was extra dead."

"Mark doesn't own me."

"No," Jack agreed. "He doesn't own you, but he loves you. And you love him." His unflinching stare pinned her in place. Daring her to acknowledge the truth.

"He doesn't love me." She faced the bar again. "And I don't love him." Jack covered her trembling hand with his work-roughened palm. "I don't want to love him." Her drink swam in her vision. "What's wrong with me, Jack? Why can't I be wanted for who I am and not for what someone else wants me to be? Drew tried to beat me into becoming his perfect woman. Mark was much nicer about trying to fit me into his vision. I don't know which one hurts more."

Jack bit back a curse. "Come here, honey."

His arms surrounded her, offering comfort and friendship. Oh, she hated this weakness. Hated that her self worth was tied to the opinion of a man. She was stronger than that. She should be stronger than that.

"There is nothing wrong with you, Gabriella." Jack spoke softly in her ear. "You are an intelligent, beautiful, strong woman. You are perfect the way you are. And Mark knows that. I'm positive that right now he is kicking his ass for hurting you. I'd be, if I were him."

Gabriella closed her eyes and took solace in his words. Why couldn't she have fallen for Jack? He was so laid back. No expectations, no ghosts of lost loves past. But no, she had to love a man whose emotions ran so deep, he appeared to stand still.

"I wish I could believe you." She sniffed lightly and pulled away.

He pushed a lock of her hair behind her ear. "You do. You're just letting hurt make you doubt. Now keep in mind that I'm not defending the man. You have every right to be a little angry. In fact, you have every right to have a little payback."

"Payback?"

A wicked gleam sparkled in his eyes. His lips curled in a way she was certain made many women hot under their skirts. "Payback, as in a little torture."

"Why would you want me to torture him?"

"Look, Mark's a great guy, but he's so damn stiff. I think he's too serious, and he thinks I'm not serious enough. You have gone a long way in removing the stick from his ass. In fact, some of my most favorite moments are courtesy of you. Aw man, when Rafe jumped off his horse to pummel the snot out of Mark? Classic. Those rash burns on his wrists from when you tied him up? Yeah, I'll remind him of that forever." He chuckled, relishing the memories.

Despite her embarrassment at being reminded that the most erotic experience of her life was public knowledge, she couldn't help but return his infectious smile. "What are you suggesting?"

His smile widened. He caught the bartender's attention, pointed to a bottle on the rack against the wall and held up two fingers again. "I suggest you have that good time that you're looking for. A real good time. Let him wonder where you are for a while."

Two shots of tequila, a saltshaker, and lime wedges were set in front of them. Slow and easy, Jack lifted his hand and tangled his fingers in the hair along her neck and tugged, tilting her head back. His warm breath tickled the sensitive skin of her neck a second before he ran his tongue over her thudding pulse. Instead of sexual shivers, his touch made her giggle in the same way she did every time he tried one of his smooth moves on her.

He picked up the shaker and shook salt on the damp spot. "Let's remind him of what he could lose by not taking care of his girl."

Could she do that? Flirt with Jack to make Mark jealous? Was that even what she wanted? The memory of how he moaned Greta's name while his cock pulsed in her mouth rang in her ears.

She lifted the lime wedge and raised a brow. Jack quickly downed the tequila and fastened his mouth on her neck, his tongue swirled and licked, making her laugh again. When she fed him the lime, he smiled around the wedge.

Yes, there was a hint of desire in his eyes, but also laughter and a conspiratorial camaraderie.

"So what do you say, Ms. Montoya?"

She lifted her shot glass. "Lead the way, Mr. Cannon."

Chapter Twenty-One

THREE HOURS. IT had been three long hours since Gabriella stormed off in a fit of rage and hurt. Three hours that Mark waited with a hair-thin patience for her to cool off. The time for waiting was over.

The kitchen in the main house was empty when he strode through. Dinner had long since been over, and the scent of whatever deliciousness that had been consumed had been replaced with the lemony scent of dish soap and surface cleaners. He marched straight up the steps to the guest room Gabriella had used and found the door wide open.

Stomping back down the stairs, he drew up short when he reached the living room. Damn. He hadn't expected everyone to be there watching the Mariners game. Didn't anyone ever leave the ranch and have a social life? The only one missing was Jack.

"Hey, man." Rafe jerked his head in greeting. "Where's Lita?"

Of course, that would be the first question anyone asked. "Hey, y'all. Greta, can I talk to you for a second?" he asked, ignoring Rafe's question. Maybe Greta had seen her.

Greta gave him a dismissive once-over. "No."

Ah, now why did he have a suspicion that she had seen her? And that she knew about what happened. Fuck.

His nostrils flared. "Please, Greta. I really need to talk to you."

This time she glared at him with her mouth pinched tight as she gritted out, "No way."

Yep. She knew. Double fuck.

Rafe got to his feet. "Where's Lita, Mark?"

Mark looked at Rafe then at the rest of the ranch hands as everyone turned away from the game to watch them with avid interest. He took a few steps to the side, placing the couch between him and Rafe.

"I'm not sure," he admitted.

Rafe's brows lowered. "Why not?"

"Because...she, huh, didn't tell me."

His thick brows lowered in warning. "What's going on?"

"I'm sorry, Rafe, but I'm not into sharing details of our relationship with you."

A thunderous expression twisted Gabriella's brother's face as he lunged, almost clearing the couch with a howl as Ben snatched him back. "What did you do, you son of a bitch?"

Adam nudged Colby. "I'm glad Ben's around this time." They both leaned back, ready to watch the fireworks display.

"What did you do?" Rafe continued to snarl and struggle against Ben's hold.

"Look." Mark kept his voice low. "We had a little argument, Gabriella took off, and I gave her time to cool off. Now all I want is to talk to her." He turned to Greta and let his desperation show in his eyes. "Where is she?"

All eyes turned in her direction. She sat with her hands clasped together and her lower lip tucked between her teeth. In the background, the Ms scored a run and the crowd cheered with excitement. A moment later, the theme song from *Bonanza* blared from Trey's pocket. He withdrew his cell and answered the call in a low tone, his attention riveted on the drama unfolding before him.

"Greta, please," Mark asked again, his voice breaking.

Her brow puckered and he could see it in her eyes that she wanted to tell him. "I don't know."

His breath started coming faster. "Please."

"I don't know. Really. She wouldn't tell me."

"Did she say anything?" Panic crawled from his belly and squeezed around his chest. Where could she have gone? The thought of her driving around made him sweat. It was dark out and the roads were long and empty. If she went into a ditch, he'd never forgive himself.

"She did say," Greta in a small voice, "that she was going to go have a good time."

Shit. That sounded like nothing but trouble.

"Where would she have gone?" There were only a few places in Mission she could have gone, unless she left town.

"I know where she is," Trey said as he tucked his phone back in his pocket.

"Where?" Mark asked. By the frown pulling Trey's mouth down, he didn't know if this was good news or bad news.

Trey swallowed then glanced back and forth between him and Rafe. "That was Mike down at the Crescent. He thought I might like to know that Gabriella was there." He swallowed again. "With Jack."

A mixture of amusement and disbelief made Mark's stomach roll. "What does that mean? Why did you say it that way, *With Jack?*"

No, no, no. She wouldn't. He wouldn't. Not if the bull rider wanted to live.

"Apparently they're putting on quite the display."

Mark shook his head and the tips of his ears burned hot.

"He wouldn't touch her."

Trey shrugged. "I'd call doing body shots touching."

Silence detonated in the room.

"I'll kill him," he snarled at the same time Rafe exclaimed, "Son of a bitch."

They raced each other to the front door and drew up short as Trey took his life into his own hands by throwing himself in front of them.

"Hold up, hold up. You can't just go charging down there."

"Why the hell not?" Mark growled.

"Gabriella is her own woman and can do what she wants. What happened between you two, anyway?"

The heat in his ears moved to his cheeks with his shame. "I said something that hurt her feelings. I didn't mean it, and I want to apologize. But that doesn't give Jack the right to touch my woman!" he exploded. The mere thought of another man touching her had him seeing red.

Rafe pushed him roughly on the shoulder. "What did you say to her?"

"That would be up to Gabriella to tell you," he replied and pushed back.

"Boys!" Trey shouted. "I'm not gonna let you go down there and cause more trouble. I'm going with you to make sure things stay civilized. Ben?"

"I'm with you, boss." His deep voice rumbled, ready to be the muscle that would keep Jack alive.

"This is going to be good," Adam snickered and followed the agitated mob to the driveway. He jumped into the flatbed of Trey's truck with Colby following while the others climbed into the cab.

Greta pressed a kiss to Trey's lips before he closed his door. "Be careful."

"I will, magpie. It's Jack you should be worried about."

GABRIELLA STUMBLED OUT of the Crescent Moon. Her heel caught in the gravel, twisting her ankle, but the liquor she had imbibed made her deceptively warm and feeling no pain. "Doesn't anyone believe in pavement in this town?" She laughed and leaned against Jack, who wrapped a strong arm around her waist.

"Hang on there, honey. We don't want you falling flat on that pretty face of yours." He chuckled and guided her to his truck.

"Shouldn't we call Ben to come get us?" She knew the big, quiet cowboy wouldn't ask questions.

"Naw, I'm sober. You were the one doing most of the drinking, while I enjoyed the flush on your cheeks and the way you danced."

She laughed and burrowed closer to his heat, letting him all but carry her across the parking lot. It had been so long since she just let loose and had a good time. No wondering about how the night was going to end. No worrying about what she said, if she sucked in her stomach enough, if she flirted the right way. The night made a turn that wasn't about seducing Jack, or anyone else, for that matter. It was about forgetting. A stolen moment to forget about everything. The time would come soon enough to fall back into the mess of reality.

When they reached his truck, Jack opened the passenger door and helped her onto the seat. "Why the sad face, darling? I thought you were having fun."

"I did, I am. I had a really good time. Thank you." She bit her lip and looked down at her hands resting in her lap. "I just— I just don't want to go home."

"I understand." He tucked her hair behind her ear. "You don't have to go back to Mark's. I'm sure you can stay at the main house."

She was already shaking her head. "I don't—"

Facing Greta again was too painful. She didn't blame the other woman for Mark's feelings, but it was still too raw to be in the same space as the woman.

"You can stay with me," he offered.

"What about Rafe?" Yeah, let's add her hotheaded brother to the mix.

"I know," Jack said with a snap of his fingers. "We'll hide out at Ben and Colby's. No one will think to look for you there."

"You think they'll let me?"

"Don't worry. I'll take care of it." He winked.

"Thanks, Jack. Your friendship means a lot to me." She threw her arms around his neck and hugged tight.

"Anytime, Gabriella."

She glanced up and became mesmerized by the moonlight highlighting his high cheekbones and square-cut jaw. Before she gave it much thought, she pressed her lips to his. His firm lips curled into a smile as he allowed her take the lead and nibble at his mouth, enjoying his lime and salt taste. It was nice, but...

"Wow," she breathed as she pulled away, eyes wide with shock.

That charming smile turned rueful. "You didn't feel a damned thing, did you?"

"No." She almost wailed as the muscles in her face fought the urge to crumple. "He's ruined me for anyone else."

Jack's laugh rumbled low in his chest. "It's gonna be all right, sweetheart. Let's get you someplace to sleep on it. Tomorrow will be much better."

He tucked her legs into the cab and closed the door. She

leaned her head back against the seat with a moan. God, she was so confused. She loved Mark with everything in her, and she wanted to believe that he felt the same way about her, but now there was doubt. And she could not live the rest of her life with Greta's shadow between them. The stress would drive her insane.

A yelp and a thud caught her attention. Peering out the windows, she saw nothing out of the ordinary, yet she couldn't see Jack either.

"Jack?" She opened the door and stuck her head out.

"Gabriella, don't—" His warning broke off with the smack of something solid hitting metal.

She turned her head in the direction of his shout and saw him behind the truck, struggling with a much taller man. Gabriella froze in shock as Jack head butted the stranger. The bigger man stumbled back a few steps, then shook his head and pulled back his fist, slamming it hard into Jack's stomach.

"Jack!" she screamed and rushed toward him with no plan as to how to help him.

She took two steps and was grabbed from behind and yanked back. She kicked and fought against the arm holding her tight, clawing at the hand that covered her mouth. Whoever was holding her, grunted in her ear as she bucked and shifted her weight to try to throw him off balance. Raising her knee, she drove her spiky heel hard into his instep.

He howled and released his hold enough for her to push free. She rounded the flat bed of the truck in time to see Jack get struck across the face. He went down hard, blood flying from his mouth and nose in a dark spray.

"Jack!" She fell to her knees by his motionless form.

Oh my God. This was not happening. This was not happening!

"Get away from him," she shouted and threw herself across

his body.

"It's not him we're after, sweetheart."

The man who hit Jack grabbed her by the hair and pulled her to her feet, covering her mouth as she screamed. She fought and spit as hard as she could, biting down on the fleshy part of the palm covering her mouth.

"Ow! Stupid bitch! Just get it done already," the one holding her down ordered his partner.

A man stepped over Jack's body and into the light of the streetlamp.

Kyle? What the hell was the college buddy of her ex-husband doing in Mission?

That motherfucker. She should have known that asshole was involved.

Fear and adrenaline filled her veins and she kicked and fought harder. Fought for her and for Jack. Where was every-body? Didn't anyone hear her scream?

She kicked out and her stiletto shoe flew off, striking the advancing bully in the groin. That little victory shot a bolt of energy through her, giving her the strength to keep up the fight.

"Fucking whore," Kyle slurred. He staggered toward her and ripped her out of the other man's hold to backhand her.

The force of the slap sent stars dancing in her vision. She was positive it would have knocked her out if he weren't still reeling from getting his balls smashed.

"Enough!" Drew stepped out from between two cars. He looked crisp and expensive in his black leather blazer, gray cashmere sweater, and pressed slacks. "Finish her."

Of course he'd leave it to his lackeys to do his dirty work.

Kyle grabbed onto her leg, his fingers biting into her thigh as he reached into his pocket. When the lamp light hit the syringe in his hand, she bucked hard. He used his teeth to pull the top off and spat it onto the ground before he jammed the needle into her thigh.

Oh God, what were they injecting her with?

"I'm going to love fucking you," Kyle growled and spat in her face. The glint in his eyes left her with no doubt that whatever he planned was going to be painful.

Her heart was going to explode, she just knew it. His leering face blurred and twisted and her lungs burned so badly that she thought flames would burst from her chest.

Run. Run!

If only she could, but her arms felt like Jell-O and the only sound coming from her lips was a feeble groan.

Kyle and his partner hauled her to the car where Drew was waiting and tossed her onto the backseat. The last thing she saw before they closed the door was Jack's unmoving body on the gravel.

No, please, God no!

Chapter Twenty-Two

MARK WAS OUT of the truck before Trey pulled to a hard stop in front of the Crescent Moon. Gabriella's Mercedes was parked near the front. He didn't know if that was a good sign or a bad one. Scanning the lot for signs of Jack's truck, he relaxed a bit when he saw the dusty Dodge two rows over.

Great, they were still there. For now. He frowned when he saw that the dome light was on. Damn, they were leaving. Together.

He raced to stop them, the others following closely on his heels. When he got his girl home, he was going to beg her for forgiveness then yell the roof down for scaring him that way.

Annoyance turned into disbelief then white-knuckle fear as he approached the truck to find Jack rolling around on the ground looking like a turtle stuck on his back. His face was swollen and blood pooled at his mouth and nose. His knuckles were swollen and bloody and the gravel around them was all torn up with evidence of a scuffle.

"What the hell?" Adam exclaimed when he caught up.

Trey quickly got on his cell and called for an ambulance while Colby fell to his knees and began to examine Jack. With a few years of vet school under his belt, he was their closest resource for medical assistance.

Mark's heart began to pound as he froze, unable to comprehend the scene before him.

"What happened? Where's Lita?" Rafe's questions added credence to the fear racing through him, causing his ears to ring.

Mark searched the cab of Jack's truck. On the floor was Gabriella's purse, still zipped, nothing taken. The ringing in his ears turned to thunder.

Rafe's gaze turned frantic as he looked at the purse in Mark's hands. "Where's Lita?"

Mark couldn't answer yet as his eyes were drawn to the deep grooves in the dirt and gravel near the truck. His knees nearly gave out when he spotted the glint of silver in the light. Near the tire, half under the truck was a sparkly rhinestone stiletto. Just one.

He knew.

"Daws," he snarled. "He took her."

Silence reigned for all of two seconds before all hell broke loose.

"Goddamn motherfucker!" Rafe shouted, doubling over as if he were going to be sick.

"I'll go inside, see if anyone saw anything," Ben said then rushed away.

Trey knelt next to Colby, who was still trying to rouse Jack. "Do you think he jumped them?"

"There was more than one. Look at the marks in the ground here. She fought them."

"There are more back here too." Adam pointed behind the truck. "Do you think one jumped Jack while the other grabbed Gabriella?"

"With Daws that makes at least two or three of them that were here."

"Motherfucker!" Rafe shouted again from where he was bent

over. "Look." He held up a blue plastic cap from the ground. "What does this look like?"

"The top of a syringe," Colby answered.

Mark fell back against the truck. They drugged her. They drugged his girl and took her to God knows where, to do God knows what to her. And he let them. He didn't take care of her. He didn't protect her. He never should have let her walk away. He was such an ass.

Rafe continued to pace and shout. His curses colored the air with his own fear and sense of failure.

Ben came running back. "No one saw anything. Mike says he saw Jack and Gabriella leave about ten minutes ago. They can't have taken her far."

Jack's body jerked once before his head rolled on his neck. A pain-filled moan broke from his bloody lips.

Colby held his shoulders down as they all crowded around them. "Damn it, Jack. Lie still. Who knows what head injuries you have. And I think your ribs are broken."

His eyes opened into slits, his mouth worked open and shut. " 'ella?" he finally rasped. "Daws."

"We figured," Mark said. "Did he say where he was taking her?"

"No. Three. Of them," he wheezed. His battered hand reached out and latched on to Mark's sleeve. One of his eyes was red with broken blood vessels, but his gaze was steady as he met Mark's stare. "Are you sorry?" he whispered.

Mark frowned at the question then understanding struck. Jack knew what happened earlier. "I'll be sorry for the rest of my life. I love her."

Jack's hold on his sleeve relaxed. "Figured that. She loves you. Sorry. I failed her."

"Stop." Mark held up his hand. He didn't know if Jack's words made him feel better or worse. "Don't make things harder on yourself. I failed. Once. I'm not going to fail again."

The brief bout of helplessness left, and in its place icy determination straightened his spine and hardened his resolve. He was not going to stand by and let that bastard take his girl without a fight.

"Rafe, Rafe, man. Come on." Mark stood in front of the dejected man and grabbed him by the arms. All of the fear and terror that gripped Mark by the balls was reflected on the face of the only other person who truly loved Gabriella. "We're going to get her. Listen to me." He gave him a shake. "We're going to get her. We're not going to let her down. She needs you."

Rafe blinked and his gaze slowly cleared. "Right. Right. We'll get her back."

They all turned at the sound of the ambulance roaring down the street. The scream of the siren launched them into action.

"Rafe. Do you have any idea where he'd take her?" Trey asked.

"I've been to their house twice, but I don't think he'd take her there. Too obvious."

"Does he have any other property?"

"Maybe a cabin. I don't know." Panic quickened his breathing and his gaze darted around as if the Dodges and Chevys in the parking lot held the answers.

"Okay, this is what we'll do." Trey took command. "Colby, you ride with Jack to the hospital. Mark, you, Rafe, Ben, and Adam will chase after Daws. If there are three of them, there should be four of you. I'll head home and search the 'Net to see what properties Daws has, and any other relatives who might be in the area. I'll also call the sheriff, have him get hold of law enforcement over in the city. Even if Daws isn't at home, they can at least search the house, maybe find a clue."

Mark clapped Rafe on the back. "Let's go get her."

Chapter Twenty-Three

THE SENSATION OF ice searing her hot cheek woke Gabriella from a fitful slumber. At either side of her head, her arms lay like sandbags and her fingers tingled. Her stomach pitched and her vision blurred in and out as she slowly lifted her eyelids.

Before her, a Tiffany lamp sat on a nightstand and glowed with a soft light, scattering a kaleidoscope of blues and greens on the cream-colored wall. The curtains to the bay window were open, revealing a slate-gray sky that made it difficult to determine the time of day. A matching dresser was against the wall, and a wooden straight-back chair was in the corner. To her frustration, not a single picture or personal item was in her field of vision.

Where the hell was she? Most certainly this was not at the home she had shared with Drew. So where had he taken her? More important, what did they do to her while she was knocked out?

The only aches and pains she carried were in her arms, wrists, and face, but that didn't mean they hadn't molested her somehow. There was no doubt in her mind that, sooner or later, Drew or one of his friends was going to rape her. Or worse.

And then there was Jack. She bit her lip to hold in her whimper. *Please let Jack be all right.* Someone had to have come after them when they never returned home. He had to have been found.

Please don't let him be dead. Please don't let him be dead.

If he died, she would never forgive herself.

"Good morning."

Gabriella jerked her head toward the feminine voice and winced with the movement. When the jolt of pain settled to a dull ache, she blinked to clear her vision. Then blinked again. And again.

Okay... She was either dreaming or her situation just had become a nightmare that took a wicked turn for the worse, if that was even possible.

Caroline Daws, Drew's mother, sat next to her on the bed with an ice pack. Her lips pursed together as she reapplied the bundle to Gabriella's cheek.

"What are you doing?" she whispered.

Caroline raised an imperious brow. "I'm tending to your wounds."

"Why? And why am I handcuffed?" Fear and uncertainty kept her voice to a low tremor.

The older woman tsked. "Well, we can't have you running around with bruises on your face, can we?"

Gabriella's teeth began to chatter as her panic soared. "Let me go."

Caroline placed the linen-wrapped ice on a plate on the nightstand. Her cool blue eyes, so similar to her son's, narrowed. "You will be released when Drew says so."

And just like that, any hope that Caroline would be an ally in helping her to escape was squashed beneath the heel of her ex-mother-in-law's sensible two-inch-high pump.

Although Gabriella wasn't really that surprised. Gaining Caroline Daws's favor had always been nearly impossible for her to achieve. Stepford Wives only wished to achieve the level of perfection and snobbery Caroline maintained with a mere blink of her eye. The woman was always coiffed and polished in the finest of clothes with a half-smile permanently curving her lips. As the wife of a successful heart surgeon, she had been the perfect hostess at all charity events and fundraisers, giving all of her attention to supporting his career and the lifestyle it provided. When her husband passed away, all of that devotion switched to her one and only son. The platinum child who could do no wrong.

Well, this time the man had done more than wrong. The egomaniac went right off the cliff.

"Caroline, Drew's breaking a million laws right now. You don't want him to go to jail, do you?"

"Drew will not go to jail. I saw the photos from the police report. It's such a shame how you tripped and fell that night. You really shouldn't have had so much to drink."

"I wasn't drunk." Anger strengthened Gabriella's voice. "He tried to sell me to his friends."

"I'm sure he had his reasons."

Holy hell. "Let me go!"

Caroline reached out and twisted her nipple hard. The pain along with the unexpected and malicious touch made her shout.

"My son gave you everything, you filthy piece of trash," she spat. "And this is how you repay him? Incarceration? Humiliation? I told him your background would be his downfall, but he was insistent that your lack of parentage and education made you the perfect pet. And I will admit, you are quite beautiful," she said with a curl of her lip. "But you are ungrateful and you owe him. So you are going to retract every bad thing you have said about Drew and you will beg him for his forgiveness. You will no longer do or say anything to further embarrass him or his family. Then you are going to take your place behind him as his dutiful wife. It's the least you can do to thank him, for the way he raised you above your station."

Gabriella stared at her former mother-in-law in horror as she realized she was going to die. There was no other possible outcome because she wasn't going to give in without the monster of all fights. And judging by the crazy gleam in Caroline's eyes, fists were going to fly.

Tears filled her eyes as her last memory of Mark came to mind. It was the first time she had ever seen his cool, unflappable resolve crumble. He was a rock, her rock, and right then she needed him, needed his strength and love so badly. To never hold him again, or kiss him...

"I see Sleeping Beauty is awake," Drew drawled as he sauntered into the room. He appeared freshly showered and dressed in a blue and white striped polo shirt and tan slacks as if he was ready for a golf date. The scent of his aftershave tickled her nose, making her eyes water even more.

"Drew, darling, you have to stop hitting her where the bruises will show," his mother scolded.

"It wasn't me. Kyle got a little hot last night."

"Speaking of whom, where is he now?"

"He went home, but will be back later tonight for his payment." He winked at Gabriella.

Message received.

Caroline shook her head. "Tell him he'll have to wait to have her. According to her medical records I obtained from Dr. Phillips, her periods are regular. I took her temperature last night and again today, and it's elevated, and her cervix is soft. I say she's ovulating, and without her birth control pills, she should be ripe. Impregnate her and use the child to make her do as you wish. Now, what can I make you for breakfast?"

What? The? Fuck? How does she know about her cervix? Ice filled Gabriella's veins as her stomach lurched. Any hope of surviving this ordeal without shedding blood was gone. Completely, totally destroyed.

Drew batted his lashes. "Will you make me eggs Benedict?"

"Of course, sweetheart." She cupped his cheeks and placed a kiss on his lips that lasted way longer than was appropriate. With a satisfied smirk, she left Gabriella alone with Satan.

A cruel smile slowly curled his lips as a menacing light entered his eyes.

Ding-ding. Round one was on.

Gabriella fueled her gaze with all of the rage seething inside her and jangled the handcuffs against the bed frame. "So what trashy movie were you watching when you hatched up this plan?"

"Ah, Gabby, I have missed seeing you in my bed." He swept his hand up from her belly to her breast.

"Don't touch me." The cuffs bit roughly into her wrists as she bucked and jerked, desperate to put any distance between them.

He laughed at her weak attempt, for they both knew she was well and truly trapped. "This is what I love most about you. All this passion. Don't you remember how good it was, baby? How we burned together. You were always so hot for me. So ready for a good fuck."

"Get your fucking hands off me!"

He slapped her across the breasts. "You belong to me!" he roared.

"You'll never get away with this," she panted through the pain. "Rafe will never stop looking for me. And Mark will tear you apart with his bare hands."

"Yes, Mark," he hummed. "Which one was he? The one you

clung to at that hoedown, or the one you were practically fucking in that bar? You hypocritical whore. I offered you men with power and you spread your thighs for those Neanderthals?"

He shoved his hands between her legs and under her skirt. The fabric cut into her skin as his fingernails scratched her as she struggled against her bonds.

"Did you fuck all of them?" he shouted over her screams. "How many men have come inside your pussy? You are mine to do with as I please. *Mine!*"

And still she fought. She pushed the pain aside and jerked until her voice was raw from the screams and blood ran down her wrists.

"You're so fucking hot when you fight me." His eyes glowed blue with his anger as he stood as he crawled onto the bed. He reached for the towel of ice and pushed the cloth into her mouth.

"Don't bother to fight me, baby," he said, laughing as he pinned down her right leg.

Like a fish on a line, she wiggled and bowed her back then thrust her hips up, swinging her left leg up to knock him in the head.

The kick wasn't as powerful as she wanted, but it connected with enough force to knock him off balance. He tumbled to the side, his hands reaching for the comforter but missing by millimeters. As he fell out of her line of vision she heard a *crack* that sounded as if bone met solid furniture.

Her chest heaved as she breathed through her nose and lay still, straining to hear over the pounding of her heart, yet there was nothing. No curse, no moan, nothing.

Did she kill him or merely knock him out? Didn't matter. Unless she found a way to get out of the cuffs, she was dead for certain once his mother returned.

Chapter Twenty-Four

MARK'S JAWS ACHED as he chewed the last piece of gum he'd been working on for nearly four hours. He ran his hand through his hair and swore he felt the prickly coarseness of the new gray strands that were sprouting with every minute that passed without word about Gabriella.

The detective handling her case had been Johnny-on-the-spot about looking for Daws to bring him in for questioning, but the fucker was nowhere to be found. The police weren't giving up on finding him, but gathering the paperwork to do a formal search of Daws's residence was going to take too long, in Mark's opinion. So he and Rafe had arrived at the home he used to share with Gabriella at the butt crack of dawn to do their own search of the perimeter, only to find the interior empty and dark when they peered into the windows. Disappointing, but not entirely unexpected.

The oversized, opulent home reminded Mark of all of the fancy things he could never give Gabriella, and for a second he felt a pang of shame. But then he remembered the way she had looked sitting on his front porch, all bundled up in his worn quilt with a huge smile on her face after he had taken her out for a ride on his horse.

Yeah, he might not be able to afford to buy her expensive,

sparkly jewelry or designer clothes, but he could give her his love. Love and eternal devotion. Something Drew Daws lacked in spades. And it was love that pushed him and Rafe to each location on the list Trey was able to obtain from the Internet.

Trey's list included homes owned by Daws and any family members he could track down. The third home on the list belonged to Daws's mother and was the next stop in their search.

"Holy shit," Rafe exclaimed from the passenger's seat as they drove up the driveway of the biggest home Mark had ever seen in his life.

Located in the city's poshest neighborhood, the three-story behemoth with cream siding and white shutters sat on a curved driveway with an honest to God fountain of an angel sitting on a cloud bubbling in the front. The place was so upscale Mark swore he could smell money in the air.

Rafe climbed out of the truck. "I can't believe Lita ever felt comfortable around these people."

"My guess is she didn't. Or she put up a good front and pretended like she did."

They approached the front steps and the sound of an approaching car made them both turn around.

A black SUV pulled up behind Mark's truck, and two men, one being the detective working Gabriella's case, stepped out of the vehicle before the engine was turned off. "What are you two doing here?"

"Detective Santiago," Rafe greeted. "Fancy meeting you here."

The man's frown deepened as he drew near. "What are you doing here?"

"We, uh, we're just visiting extended family."

"Right. Look, I told you we're doing everything we can to

find your sister, Mr. Montoya. I can't have you doing your own investigation and ruining mine in the process."

"And you have to understand, Detective," Mark interjected. "Our top priority is getting our girl back. In one piece. Now. Our intention is not to interfere in your police work or break the law, but make no mistake, we will not stop looking for her until she's back home with us."

"You're already breaking the law. You're trespassing." The detective's dark eyebrows lowered. "This is a gated community. How did you get onto the neighborhood?"

Rafe answered, "They took one look at us and the truck and waved us through, telling us to make sure we pick up every fallen leaf. Fucking profilers."

The other policeman burst out laughing, then choked on it when Santiago shot him a quelling look. The officer shrugged. "Sorry. But he's right."

"Get in your truck, sirs," Santiago said with a sigh. "I won't make you leave, but you can't come inside with us. I'll tell you what I can after we've asked our questions." When Mark opened his mouth to argue, the man pulled back the tails of his jacket and rested his hand on the stock of the Taser in his belt.

Mark jerked his head at the truck. "Come on, Rafe. Let's allow the man to do his job. Take all the time you need, Detective. We'll be waiting right here for you."

He backed the few feet down to his ride, and leaned against the door, his arms folded across his chest. Rafe stood beside him and rested his hand on the side of the flatbed and flashed the policemen an innocent smile.

The detective's jaw tightened before he and his partner walked up the steps to the red double doors and rang the bell. And waited. And waited.

Rafe shifted his weight while Mark cracked the knuckles in

one hand, then the other. He was about to push his way forward and pound on the damn door when it finally opened.

The slender, stately woman who answered the door had a serene, blank look on her face. Mark was certain her brows would have risen as well if not for the gallon of Botox she probably had injected into her forehead. For seven o'clock in the morning, she was quite elegantly dressed in a cream-colored silk blouse and matching slacks. Her makeup was troweled on and her hair was pulled back into a bun that was so tight it probably tided her over until her next facelift.

"Good morning. How may I help you?" Mark heard her faintly from his post by the truck.

"I'm Detective Santiago and this is Detective Peters. We're looking for Ms. Caroline Daws."

She blinked rapidly. "Why, that's me."

Hm. And here Mark thought she'd have hired help answer the door for her. Where was the butler?

"Ma'am, we're looking for your son, Drew. Do you know where we can find him?"

She glanced over the policemen's shoulders to where Mark and Rafe stood then back at the detectives as she frowned, at least as much of a frown as the Botox allowed. "I would think he's at his home. Is there something wrong? Has he been injured?"

"When was the last time you've heard from him?"

"Why, yesterday afternoon. Detective, what is this about?"

On the back of Mark's neck the tiny hairs stood on end as he noted Mrs. Daws didn't open the door all of the way, and blocked the narrow opening with her body.

"Last night his ex-wife, Gabriella, was taken. We would like to question him about it."

Her thin, manicured hand flew to her throat. "Taken? Do

you mean kidnapped? How is that possible? Drew just spoke to her yesterday."

All four men tensed at her words. Next to him, Rafe swore beneath his breath.

"Excuse me, ma'am? He spoke with her?" Santiago questioned with a disbelieving note in his voice.

"Well, yes." She blinked at the tall policeman, all wide-eyed and innocent. "He said Gabby called him yesterday and told him that she was sorry about everything that had happened and that she still loved and missed him." Mark's stomach twisted at her words. "He told me she wanted to reconcile. They were supposed to meet last night and talk things over."

Mark spat his gum into the fountain as Rafe burst out, "That's a lie."

"Who are you?" Mrs. Daws's gaze shifted to them, her eyes narrowing as disdain curled her collagen-filled lips.

Santiago lifted his hand at them in warning when Rafe took a menacing step forward. "Who they are is not important right now. Mrs. Daws, we need to speak with your son. Where might he be?"

Fire flashed in her eyes and she tilted her head. If a thought was worth a penny, Mark would bet that she had at least a grand running through her mind, and all of them were as tainted as mob money.

Suddenly, Santiago and his partner straightened in alarm and Mrs. Daws turned to look over her shoulder.

"What was that?" Santiago asked as his hand drifted toward his holster.

"Nothing." Mrs. Daws giggled oddly. "Now where were we?"

Mark's inner radar went off, and he drifted closer to the trio at the door when a muffled scream echoed down the staircase and his body jerked as if he'd been shot. "Gabriella."

Santiago beat him inside the door, but Mark was right on his coattails as they pushed past Ms. Daws, who shouted, "Wait! You cannot just barge into my home!"

Her shouts were drowned out by the men pounding up the carpeted stairs. At the top, the hallway split in two directions, with doors lining both sides.

A muffled shout and a heavy thud drew them to the left, with Mark in the lead down to the last door. With his blood roaring in his ears, he ignored Santiago's warning shouts and rushed through the open doorway, falling to his knees as he took in the sight before him.

Gabriella, his Gabriella, was cuffed to a bed. Blood ran down her arms and wetted her hair in sticky strands that clung to her cheeks. A cloth was in her mouth and the left side of her face was a sickly mottle of blues and purples. But what gutted him more than her bruises were her tears and seeing her with her skirt hiked up to her hips and scratches marring the inside of her thighs.

Who knew how long he stood, rooted to the floor. It wasn't until the clink of handcuffs against the headboard broke through his horror and spurred him into action. As he climbed on the bed, he saw the body of Drew Daws, wedged into the space between the bed and the dresser. Beneath his head, blood stained the sand-colored carpet.

Concern for the fucker didn't cross Mark's mind as he pulled the cloth free from her mouth. She immediately began coughing as she stared up at him in disbelief.

Her tongue and throat worked at bringing the moisture back to her mouth as she croaked, "Mark?"

"I'm here, darlin'. You're safe now." He brushed the hair from her face, his heart breaking.

Behind him was a stifled curse as Santiago rounded the bed with Rafe right behind. He reached for his radio. "Dispatch, this is R-113, I need medical at…"

"Gabriella, darlin', it's going to be okay." He stroked his hand over her forehead as her shaking grew worse. "Damn it. I need to get these off." He pulled at the cuffs.

"Here, try these." Santiago tossed him a set of keys as he knelt by Daws's still body.

"Is he dead?" she whispered.

"No. Just knocked cold," the detective answered.

To Mark's relief, the cuffs popped free, and he ran his hands up and down her arms. She bit back a moan as the blood rushed back into her shoulders.

Rafe squeezed onto the bed next to them and reached across her to tug the edge of the bedspread over her body.

"Rafe?" she gasped. "How?"

"Long story." Rafe laid the back of his hand against her cheek. "You're burning hot."

"Drugged me." She began to shake and her teeth chattered as she asked, "Jack?"

"He's fine." Mark nudged Rafe to get off the bed so they could enclose her in the entire comforter. "Some bruised ribs and a broken nose. He won't be as pretty, but he'll be fine." He cradled her in his arms as the tremors turned to near convulsions and her tears fell. "Gabriella, I am so sorry. I love you. I love you so much. And I'm so sorry." One of his tears mixed with hers on her cheek.

"I love you too." She tried to brush his lips with trembling fingers. "I thought I would never see you again."

"I'd never let you go that easily," he whispered, his throat tight with all of the fear he had battled over the last twelve hours still searching for a way to break free. "I love you."

"Take me home." She sagged in his arms and reached out a hand toward Rafe.

"Sure thing, darlin'. We're gonna take you to the doctor and then straight home. And I'll be with you the entire time."

Teary eyed and bruised, but she smiled, a soft smile blossoming in the most beautiful vision he'd ever seen.

"Good," she mumbled and her lashes fluttered. In seconds, she was fast asleep.

Epilogue

THE SNOW FELL so thick and heavy, it was as if the clouds were overstuffed pillows that didn't survive a night spent with a gaggle of enthusiastic twelve-year-old girls during a slumber party and exploded all over the world.

Mark settled Gabriella on his lap and tucked the heavy wool blanket tighter around them.

The view from their front porch of the paddock with the rolling hillsides of Central Washington in the background was stunning in its quiet beauty. A perfect setting for him to enjoy the miracle in his arms.

"It's so beautiful," Gabriella said, sighing and snuggling closer. "I've always loved a white Christmas."

He practically purred in agreement, but thought that nothing was more beautiful than the love he saw in her eyes.

It had been a long month for Gabriella, but she had weathered the stress with a grace and strength that made him proud to stand by her side.

Daws and his mother were awaiting trial for several charges, among them kidnapping and assault at the top of the list. Mark would rather have the entire event over and done, with the clang of the prison doors echoing in his ears as the dastardly duo was locked away forever, but he took comfort that bail was denied, and Gabriella was far away from their reach.

Mark leaned in for a kiss. Her nose was cold but her lips were soft and warm. He took his time, enjoying her texture, her taste, the way she sighed into his mouth. He'd never get enough of the smoldering heat that fired in his belly and slowly consumed every molecule of his being anytime she was near.

"I love you, Gabriella," he said in a low voice and pressed his forehead to hers.

"I love you too," she whispered. Her smile was so soft, so delicate, and full of love that his throat closed up and the moisture that pooled in his eyes stung in the cool breeze.

He tilted her chin up and gazed into her eyes. "I. Love. You. You, Gabriella. From the moment you first stepped out of that shiny Mercedes, I knew you were my woman. And I have never doubted it once. You're my world. I—" He swallowed hard at the sight of a tear spilling down her cheek. "I just love you."

Her watery smile trembled as she laid her palm against his cheek, her thumb finding his dimple. "I love you, Mark."

"I know it's a day early, but I want to give you your Christmas present now." He reached into his shirt pocket and pulled out an open packet of gum. "Hold out your hand."

"Did you have Greta make me something?" The corner of her mouth quirked up in humor.

He nipped at her chin. "Not this time."

Very carefully, he upended the package over her upturned hand. A ring slid out as silent as the snow falling around them. Gabriella gasped and stared at the antique diamond ring in her palm.

"It was my grandmother's," he murmured. Behind his ribs, his heart beat like a stampede and sweat beaded over his lip. "I don't expect an answer right away, but I just wanted to let you know that I want forever with you. And I'd really like to be your husband."

She giggled and sniffed at the same time. "That's good because I would very much like to be your wife." She slipped the ring on her finger.

"Yeah?" His cheeks burned from the combination of cold and his huge smile.

"Yeah."

Mark soaked in the love in her kiss and the heat in her touch as she melted against him.

"This is the best Christmas ever," she said against his lips. "Do you think anyone will notice if we're really late for breakfast tomorrow?"

"Breakfast? Hell, darling, they may not see us until New Year's."

Her delighted laughter skipped out into the twilight before being swallowed up by his kiss.

His woman was right.

Best Christmas ever.

About Anna Alexander

Anna Alexander's literary world changed at age thirteen when a friend gave her Kathleen E. Woodiwiss' *A Rose in Winter*. With her mind thoroughly blown, Anna decided that one day she too would become a romance novelist. With Hugh Jackman's abs and Christopher Reeve's blue eyes as inspiration, she loves spinning tales about superheroes finding love.

The Cloudy skies over her Pacific Northwest home give her plenty of opportunity to indulge in her passions, which are reading, writing and snuggling with a steaming cup of Irish coffee. Now if she could only find a hot Irishman to go with it, then life would be perfect.

Anna welcomes comments from readers.

Website
http://annaalexander.net/

Facebook
https://www.facebook.com/pages/Anna-Alexander/282170065189471?ref=hl

Twitter
https://twitter.com/AnnaWriter

Newsletter
http://eepurl.com/Q0tsz

ALSO BY ANNA ALEXANDER

Men of the Sprawling A Ranch Series

The Cowboy Way

The Marlboro Man

Heroes of Saturn Series

Hero Unmasked

Hero Rising

Cavern Series

A Night at The Cavern

www.ingramcontent.com/pod-product-compliance
Lightning Source LLC
Chambersburg PA
CBHW050933120626
46552CB00001B/190